Praise for Finding Isobel

~

An eventful story of an intrepid adoptee discovering her background and gaining strength for her future.
~ Kirkus

The compelling story of a young woman battling to discover who she is and where she's from. Highly recommended. The author is a talented writer who is excellent at keeping the reader immersed in the story.
~ The Wishing Shelf

An absorbing and poignant novel about a woman's search for identity and path in life, Finding Isobel *by Mary Behan examines the complex and painful choices that can rip families apart, as well as the kind, loving choices that can bring families together. Written with intimacy and realism,* Finding Isobel *is a probing story about what it means to belong, asking and answering deep questions about life and the meaning of family, for a truly moving work of contemporary fiction.*
~ Self-Publishing Review

Writing with a profound sense of insight, perceptive observation, and attention to detail, Behan captures the overwhelming impact of love and loss on human connections in times of turmoil. This delicately crafted tale of love and loss packs an emotional punch.
~ BookviewReview

Wholly original, clear-eyed, and fierce, Mary Behan's Finding Isobel *is infused with humanity's instinctive longing for home, a knowledge of who we are and where we come from. Behan writes with a deep sense of compassion, yet she has produced a propulsive page-turner that is global in scope, a beautiful tale of one woman's drive and will to know.*

~ Barry Wightman, Award-Winning Author of *Pepperland* and president of the Wisconsin Writers Association.

This is a fast-paced, compelling narrative that takes the reader along for the ride. It is a novel-reading experience unlike any other and guaranteed to keep you focused with every truth Isobel survives along the way. Read this book now.

~ Laurie Scheer, Writing Mentor, Developmental Editor, Mediagoddess

From the first pages of Finding Isobel, *I knew I was in the hands of a master storyteller. This is a heart-felt story of love, longing, frustration, and the search for answers, not only about Isobel's past but about her future. Isobel is one of those captivating characters who stayed with me long after I finished the novel. Well done, Mary Behan.*

~ Gregory Lee Renz, International Award-Winning Author of *Beneath the Flames*

Readers will be mesmerized by this beautifully written story of Isobel's journey as she unlocks the secrets of her past. Finding Isobel goes beyond a riveting, page-turning story to explore what it means to be a parent, a child, and the effects that secrets and decisions cause throughout lives.

~ Kathy Steffen, Author of the Award-Winning *Spirit of the River* Series

Also by Mary Behan

Abbey Girls
(co-author Valerie Behan)

A Measured Thread

Kernels

FINDING ISOBEL

Mary Behan

Laurence Gate Press

No part of this book may be reproduced in any form or by any means without permission from the author.

You can contact the author at mvbehan.com

Publisher's Cataloging-in-Publication Data
Names: Behan, Mary, author.
Title: Finding Isobel / Mary Behan.
Description: Mazomanie, WI: Laurence Gate Press, 2024.
Identifiers: ISBN978-1-7344943-6-5 (paperback) | ISBN978-1-73449-43-7-2 (ebook) | ISBN978-1-7344943-8-9 (audio book)
Subjects: LCSH: Women--Fiction. | Family--Fiction. | Mother-daughter relationship--Fiction. |Adoption--Fiction. | New Zealand--Fiction. | Bosnia and Herzegovina--Fiction. | BISAC:FICTION / Women. |FICTION / Family Life / General.
Classification: LCCPS3602.E33 F56 2024 (print) | LCCPS3602.E33 (ebook) | DDC813 / .6--dc23.

LCCN: 2028917828

Copyright 2024 by Mary Behan
All rights reserved

Cover image "Finding Joy" by Gina Hecht
♦ ginahecht.com

Cover and interior design by CKBooks Publishing
♦ ckbookspublishing.com

Laurence Gate Press
6383 Hillsandwood Rd.
Mazomanie, WI 53560

Fiction is the great lie that tells the truth about how the world lives!

~ Abraham Verghese, *The Covenant of Water*

CHAPTER 1

Isobel considered her options: call 911 or let Maggie die.

That morning she had dropped Oliver off at Maggie's house before going to work. Immediately she opened the door to the old log cabin, the dog rushed past her and made a beeline upstairs to the bedroom where Isobel knew he would jump on the bed and smother the elderly lady with wet kisses. She called out a brief hello and waited for Maggie's usual response. Nothing. She called again, louder this time in case Maggie was still asleep. She could hear Oliver whining upstairs, a high-pitched repetitive sound as if he were in pain. Stepping inside, she made her way to Maggie's bedroom. Oliver was standing on his hind legs at the side of the bed, one paw resting on the quilt, the other scratching excitedly at the air. She gently pushed the dog aside and leaned in closer, trying to detect any sign of a breath. It was there, barely disturbing the sheet Maggie had pulled up to her chest. The old woman's thin, liver-spotted hands rested lightly on the quilt, its faded blue and white squares barely visible in the dim light. Isobel stroked her wrist tenderly, reassured that it was still warm. She counted the shallow breaths. In the space of a minute there were five, barely enough to keep someone alive.

Ever since Maggie had returned from Ireland six months earlier, Isobel had tried to brace herself for the inevitable. Maggie O'Connor had terminal cancer, and the magical interlude of the past fifteen months was coming to an end. She had visibly slowed. Nonetheless, each morning Maggie would grab her hiking poles and take the dog for a walk around the prairie, stopping ever more frequently at the benches Vic had placed along the mown path. After her walk, she would make a cup of tea and take it to the screen porch, settling into an old rocking chair with Oliver at her feet. Isobel had spent countless hours here with Maggie, learning how to embrace life. Maggie had given Isobel a home and a family and saved her from her demons. Now there would be no more walks, no more shared cups of tea.

Isobel looked around the familiar room. A large white envelope was propped up on the dresser with the words SUICIDE NOTE scrawled across the front in block letters. She thought about opening the envelope but decided against it. What would happen if she were accused of assisting this suicide?

An empty wine glass stood on Maggie's nightstand — its bottom caked with white dregs — along with two envelopes, one addressed to Isobel herself and the other to Vic, Isobel's boyfriend; these too she left untouched. Careful not to touch the glass, she sniffed but didn't detect any odor other than wine. She called Oliver away and with a final look around the bedroom, went downstairs and let herself out of the cabin. Walking the short distance to the guesthouse she and Vic shared, she paused to look at the sea of tall grasses interspersed with yellow and purple flowers that stretched westward toward a large pond. On this early July morning with the prairie at its peak, Isobel acknowledged that Maggie had chosen the perfect time to kill herself.

When she opened the door to the guesthouse, Oliver was reluctant to go inside. Instead, he turned and began to run back to the cabin.

"No, you're not going to see Maggie. Not now," she said, calling the dog back.

Hearing the woman's name spoken aloud, she let out a sob, then quickly suppressed it. Ignoring the dog's plaintive whines, she shut herself in the bathroom. She needed to think.

∽

Sitting on the toilet seat, Isobel closed her eyes and began to take slow, deep breaths, focusing on scenarios that would inevitably play out over the next hours, days, and weeks. If she called 911, an ambulance would arrive in less than fifteen minutes, its siren echoing throughout the valley, alerting everyone that something was amiss down the long gravel driveway that led to Maggie's cabin. Despite the suicide note, Isobel was sure the EMTs would intubate and ventilate the old lady before rushing her to the nearest hospital. That was their job, after all. If Maggie regained consciousness and could be weaned off the ventilator, she would be sent to a nursing home. At eighty years of age and with a terminal disease, this would be seen as the kindest intervention, especially as she lived alone. Even if hospice was an option, Maggie had already made clear she didn't want to prolong her life. Having seen her almost daily for the past fifteen months, Isobel was keenly aware of the older woman's wish to die in her own home — a settler's log cabin nestled into a hillside facing a tallgrass prairie in southwestern Wisconsin where she had lived for the past fifty years. She would never forgive Isobel for thwarting her suicide.

Isobel calculated that if she waited a few more hours, time would take care of the situation. Although she wasn't certain how much of the drug Maggie had taken, she was sure the dose had been carefully calculated and would eventually have its desired effect. Working at a veterinary clinic, Isobel had watched enough dog and cat euthanasia to know what happens when breathing slows to the point where it can no longer sustain life. As the drug made its way through blood vessels, you watched the animal's chest rise and fall, slowing with each breath until the movement was imperceptible. The owner's crying typically slowed too, from heaving sobs to a single line of tears coursing down each blotched cheek. An image of Maggie lying unconscious flashed into Isobel's mind, and for a moment she had an urge to rush back to the cabin, to hold and stroke the older woman's hand just as she would an elderly dog drifting into its final sleep.

She tried to imagine life without Maggie. Ever since she had come to work for the elderly lady fifteen months earlier, she had been Maggie's constant companion. At the time Maggie had been recovering from a serious fall down her basement stairs and needed help with daily chores such as shopping and cooking, as well as chauffeuring to and from various appointments. This had coincided with Isobel's decision to leave her job as a school counselor, giving her both time and income while she considered her next move. What Isobel hadn't anticipated was how attached to Maggie she would become.

Isobel was adopted and had never discovered who her real parents were. She was born in Sarajevo, Bosnia, and had grown up in Canada with immigrant parents — a mother from New Zealand and a father from Serbia. Neither parent would disclose any details of how they had come to adopt her. As soon as she left home for the University of Wisconsin in Madison on a tennis scholarship, her parents moved to New Zealand, and over the past seven years she had rarely heard from them. Maggie had become her *de facto* family. And it was through Maggie she had met her boyfriend, Vic.

A stab of panic riveted her. How was she going to tell Vic his favorite person in the whole world was about to die? He would never forgive her for not calling the EMTs. Another thought came to her: perhaps she could suggest that he drop by Maggie's place later this evening, have him be the one to make the discovery? By then it should all be over. But the image of Vic walking into Maggie's bedroom to the scene she had just left was heartbreaking. She couldn't do that to him.

Isobel opened her eyes and took a deep breath. She had made her decision. She went through the scenario carefully, visualizing each step as if she were rehearsing an episode in a TV drama.

Chapter 2

That evening Isobel "discovered" Maggie's body. She made herself a cup of tea while she waited for the ambulance. Carrying the mug to the screen porch, she sat in her usual place on an old wicker loveseat facing Maggie's rocking chair. It seemed impossible that she would never see Maggie again, never be able to unburden herself to the wise person who reassured her that she was loved. This porch was where she had spent hours reading to Maggie the previous summer. With failing eyesight, Maggie had asked Isobel to read aloud a package of old letters — letters she had written to her parents when she first emigrated to the United States fifty years earlier. These were an extraordinary window into another time, prompting thoughtful conversations between the two women. As Isobel thought back to that summer, she realized it had been a master class in how to live a full life.

Although Isobel was itching to open the letter Maggie had left for her, she decided to wait until the police came.

~

The next few days were particularly devastating for Isobel and Vic but especially Vic. Maggie's suicide was a shock; he just couldn't comprehend why she had left without saying goodbye. She had been a part of his life since he was a young boy, accompanying his father, a carpenter, to do repairs at Maggie's place.

All the joy had been sucked out of Vic. He had gone to work each day with grim determination, returning just in time for dinner. Afterwards he went outside to do chores — mowing the fire breaks around the prairie, chopping wood, repairing equipment — anything to keep himself occupied.

∼

Vic was loading the dishwasher with his usual care, determined to fit one last plate or mug into the already full space. She had been waiting for the right moment to bring up a question she was itching to ask.

"What did Maggie say in her letter?"

The question hung in the air between them.

"It was typical Maggie...."

There was a catch in Vic's voice, and he cleared his throat before continuing.

"First, she apologized for not telling me she was going to do it. Said I'd try to stop her, try to talk her out of it."

Isobel touched him on the arm, interrupting his rearranging, and took one of his hands in hers.

"She said she'd come back to haunt me if I didn't look after this place."

He gave a quiet laugh, and they both smiled.

"Anything else?" Isobel asked, trying to sound casual.

"Just to make sure to contact her lawyer and her financial advisor. I've done that already."

He let go of her hand momentarily and closed the dishwasher. Turning to face her, she saw that his eyes were glistening. He gave a deep sigh.

"I'm not sure what happens next. This place was all sorted out last fall. The land and the buildings are definitely mine; I got the tax bill in December — ten thousand dollars!"

"But Maggie paid that, didn't she?"

"Of course she did. That was just like her, making it easy for me."

Vic was suddenly silent. Isobel imagined he was replaying pieces of his past, which since the age of five had often included Maggie.

"What's happening with Bill Breunig? Is he still going to build those houses next door?"

Isobel made a gesture with her free hand towards the neighboring property where Breunig had applied to the town board for permission to build six houses, which would be accessed by a new road passing within thirty feet of the guesthouse where she and Vic lived. Maggie had registered an objection with the county and hired a lawyer to argue her case.

"I think Bill might have given up on the idea. He's not going to be able to buy that strip of land for the driveway, and the only other access is across his own property, which is way too hilly and would be very expensive. No. Breunig's plan was all about Maggie — the road, the houses, everything. For some reason he hated her. I suppose he couldn't accept the fact that a frail eighty-year-old lady could thwart his plans. Boy, was she tough."

"So, what are you going to do now?"

"What do you mean?"

"Well…about this place. Now you've got three places to look after: the house on Highway 19 you're still renting, Maggie's cabin, and this place."

Vic frowned, scrunching up one side of his face.

"I honestly don't know. I mean, I've been thinking about it but not in any real way. I suppose I didn't want to jump ahead — think about Maggie being gone." He gave another sigh. "I don't want to rush into anything just yet."

"I know what you mean."

Isobel let go of his hand and leaned down to pat Oliver, who was looking at both of them expectantly. It was time for his evening walk.

"What about you? What was in her letter to you?" Vic asked.

"Oh, much the same," Isobel replied. "An apology because she suspected you would ask me to help you tidy up the cabin after she was gone. Sell off her furniture, like I did with the guesthouse last year."

"You mean what you did when you first came to work for her, getting rid of her husband's things? Didn't she split the proceeds with you?" His expression changed. "Hey, there's an idea. You could do the same thing with her cabin. I'll give you half of what we get for the stuff, just like she did."

"And where do you think I'm going to get the time, Vic Wagner? I start vet school in a month. And just in case you had forgotten, I still have a full-time job."

"Okay, okay," he said, raising his hands as if to deflect her anger. "But we could do it together. We could start this weekend. I know I'm useless with Craig's List or whatever you used. Just tell me what to do."

A bit irritated, Isobel countered, "I plan to clean out Maggie's fridge this weekend, get rid of perishables, do a few loads of laundry...the essentials. We could do it together." She gave him a knowing look.

Vic slapped his forehead with the heel of his hand.

"Ah, shit! I forgot. I promised to help Phil with his barn-raising this Saturday. A bunch of the guys are getting together, and I swore I'd be there. I told you weeks ago, didn't I? We think we can get it done over four Saturdays, maybe five." He gave her an apologetic look. "I'm sorry."

Isobel glared at him. This was typical of Vic. When it came to his friends, he was generous to a fault, willing to help out with any project. His skills were broad ranging, so he was always in demand. Yet, while she had never begrudged the time he devoted to Maggie, from mowing grass to clearing brush and mending miscellaneous equipment, sometimes she wanted to shout, "But what about me?"

"We could start on Sunday...?" he said tentatively.

"Forget it," she replied, grabbing her coat. "I'm going to take Oliver for a walk."

Chapter 3

Isobel pulled the copy of *A Sand County Almanac* from a shelf in the living room and withdrew Maggie's letter from between its pages. It was unlikely Vic would ever find the letter there. He wasn't much of a reader, and his choices tended towards Lee Child and John Sandford as opposed to environmental classics. She had read the letter multiple times in the previous week and by now knew it almost by heart. Yet, she found herself reading it once again, searching for answers. Maggie's letter had changed everything.

> *Dearest Isobel,*
>
> *I'm sorry I didn't say goodbye. I'm sorry too that you'll be asked to help with tidying up after me. But we both know you're good at that! You're good at so many things.*
>
> *I cannot tell you how much you have meant to me over the past year. You became my surrogate granddaughter, and together with Oliver, you filled my days with joy. Vic too, but he has always been in my life. <u>You</u> were the unexpected treasure. Despite the fact that my daughter*

and I didn't have the reunion you hoped for, without you I would never have found her. More than anything, you helped me come to terms with giving her up for adoption all those years ago. That was a priceless gift.

I know you are angry with me right now. However, if you learned anything from me over the past year, you understand that I did the right thing. You and Vic would have suffered much more had I lingered for another few months, in pain and fading in front of your eyes. This way you get to move on with your lives.

This is what I really want to talk to you about — moving on. I don't think you will ever be happy until you know who your real parents are. Just as you helped me find my daughter, I want to help you find them. I've been thinking about this quite a lot recently, how you might go about it. This is one of those times when a bit of money can help. So I've put $50,000 into your bank account. You'll be able to go to New Zealand and meet your adoptive parents. I'm hoping that when they see you, see the wonderful young woman you have become, they will be willing to tell you more. They are getting old too, and people tend to look at things differently when the years ahead are numbered.

This money is separate from what I've left you in my will. When probate is settled, you'll receive enough to pay for vet school. I'm so proud of you getting accepted, especially as I was able to watch your transition from an unhappy school counselor to an aspiring veterinarian. I wish I could be around to watch your journey, but I'll be there in your heart just as you are in mine.

With so much love,
Maggie

The idea of becoming a vet had taken some time to mature. While an undergraduate student at the university, Isobel had cleaned kennels in the veterinary hospital on weekends to supplement her tennis scholarship. On nights when the clinic was particularly busy, the residents and technicians often asked her to help them, and she found that she enjoyed working with the animals. After graduation, her degree in psychiatry with an emphasis in child behavior led her to apply for a position as a counselor at a local high school. It was a good job, but after two years Isobel realized her tolerance for helicopter parents and their whiny children was exhausted.

In the end, it was Oliver who changed her career. A year after she adopted him from the Dane County animal shelter, he'd been hit by a car, which broke his leg. Seeing the care he received at the veterinary school hospital and how devoted the faculty and staff were to his recovery, was all she needed. She left her job at the end of the school year. Soon after she met with the veterinary school director of admissions, who was very encouraging, outlining the courses she would have to take and the need for obtaining real-life experience.

As she thought back to that sequence of events, Isobel marveled at how everything had fallen into place. Once Maggie had recovered from her fall, she had let Isobel stay at the guesthouse for free in exchange for minimal assistance with housekeeping. Isobel took classes at the university and volunteered at a local veterinary clinic. She had met Vic at Maggie's place when he replaced the barn roof, and over the course of a few months, they had become a couple. On weekday mornings before going to work she dropped Oliver off at Maggie's cabin, knowing he was welcome there. The dog was company for Maggie, who still managed to take a short walk each day, hiking poles in hand. Each Friday evening, Isobel and

Vic cooked dinner for Maggie at her cabin, filling her in on the comings and goings in their lives. This was Isobel's family. But now everything was up in the air, and the one person whose advice she needed was gone.

Maggie had been right about one thing — moving on. Despite years of therapy, Isobel had never managed to overcome the feeling she had been abandoned, not just by her biological parents but her adoptive parents too. As far back as she could remember, she was aware of how little warmth her adoptive mother showed. Other mothers smiled and hugged their children when they picked them up from school, but not hers. Her father showed some affection but only when they were alone together, as if he was afraid his wife might disapprove of his misplaced allegiance. Isobel remembered a particularly emotional meeting with her therapist where she had howled "What's wrong with me?" Her despair frightened both of them. Why had her adoptive parents not loved her, her mother especially? After all, they had chosen to adopt; they could have remained childless. Was she somehow incomplete — a secondhand child?

Now, there was a chance to find out who her biological parents were, perhaps even meet them. After all, she had managed to find Maggie's daughter and reunite them. That had been the defining achievement of Isobel's past year, and each time she thought about it, a warm glow filled her. While their reunion had not been as affectionate as she expected, she was inclined not to dwell on that fact.

Maggie's letter changed everything. Now she could go to New Zealand. Once her adoptive parents saw her and recognized this was their final opportunity to make up for years of remoteness, they must surely relent and tell her everything.

Her own efforts at finding a relative had been a failure, despite uploading her DNA to 23andMe and Ancestry.com.

She would go. The question was when? Could she settle down to four years of vet school? And what if her parents died before she had a chance to confront and question them? The more she thought about it, the clearer it became. She had to go now.

~

Dr. Forrest, the director of admissions at the veterinary school, greeted her warmly and gestured towards a chair in her cramped office. A slender, tall middle-aged woman with shoulder-length dark hair, she wore a white coat embroidered with her name. Her heavy-lidded eyes were framed by glasses, making it difficult for Isobel to get a sense of how the meeting might go. She took the proffered seat and smiled, hoping to insert some warmth into their exchange.

"You must be getting excited," the professor said. "In barely three weeks you'll be here for orientation."

Isobel clasped her hands in her lap. She moistened her lips before speaking.

"Something has come up in my personal life — something extremely important — and I would like to postpone entering vet school until next year."

She could hear a note of petulance in her voice as she tried to explain, and for a brief moment she was reminded of school counseling sessions she had held with difficult pupils. Noting the look of concern on Dr. Forrest's face, her grip tightened.

"I'm very sorry Isobel, but you've left it too late." The professor shook her head abruptly from side to side.

The blunt statement stunned Isobel.

Dr. Forrest continued, her tone now formal and professional.

"It's true we grant deferments in exceptional circumstances. They are considered on an individual basis by the Admissions Committee, who then makes a final recommendation to the dean. But these requests have to be made within a month of being accepted into the program. In other words, by last May."

Dr. Forrest leaned back slightly in her chair. "If you withdraw now, you'll lose your place. You can reapply for the coming year, but you'll be treated as a new applicant, and I cannot say whether you'll be successful or not. It all depends on the strength of the applicant pool." She paused before adding, "Perhaps you need a few days to think about this. It's a big decision. However, the sooner you let us know, the better. We have a long list of students who are more than willing to take your spot. I'll give you a day, Isobel, to decide if you can make this program your priority. If not, please give the next person on the waiting list the courtesy of a quick reply."

The professor's face was unsmiling when she stood up, bringing the meeting to a close.

Isobel had gone to this meeting assuming she would be granted a deferment, her only concern being how she would explain her change of mind to Vic. But now the decision carried far more weight. She walked towards the exit, blind to people passing her in the corridor. At any other time she might have looked for familiar faces from when she was an undergraduate student working in the veterinary hospital, but not now. Her mind was in turmoil. How could she give up her place? Surely she could wait until next year to go to New Zealand. Still, her mother had mentioned in her annual Christmas card that her father was not well. What if he died? What if they both died before she had a chance to talk to them? She could apply to vet school for next year, but as Dr. Forrest pointed out, it all depended on the applicant pool. She had no idea where she ranked this year. Was she their top choice or their last? These arguments were bouncing back and forth in her head as she stepped outside into the bright sunlight.

Chapter 4

With Maggie no longer around to take care of Oliver, Isobel got up early each morning to take the dog for a walk, returning for a quick breakfast before driving to her job at the veterinary clinic. Not understanding why his routine had changed, Oliver dashed towards Maggie's cabin each morning and only reluctantly followed Isobel in the direction of the prairie. For the next half hour he followed her, occasionally leaving her side for forays into the tall grass. Sometimes he would flush a mouse, and the ensuing flurry of activity, though hidden from her, managed to bring a smile to her face.

On these morning walks Isobel often found herself talking aloud to Maggie. She could listen to how her words sounded, how they might fall on another's ears and be received. It helped with organizing her thoughts and marshalling her arguments, a rehearsal of sorts for what was to come.

"How am I going to tell him?" she asked aloud. "I know he'll disapprove. He's such a good guy, always doing the right thing. He'll tell me to get through the first year of vet school and then go, as I'll have the summer off. I haven't told him about the money you gave me for the trip. I'm not sure why. It's not as if we keep secrets from each other." Listening to what she had just said, she sighed loudly. "Until now.... I can never tell him you were still breathing when I found you that day. He wouldn't be able to forgive me. It would destroy our relationship. Better maybe to let him read your letter because you put it so well. *You* know how important this is to me. Knew. What the fuck, Maggie? Why did you have to die?"

∼

Vic's truck was gone by the time she returned from her walk. She could feel the tension leaving her shoulders, the dreaded conversation postponed. Opening the door to the guesthouse, again she had to call Oliver away from the path leading to Maggie's cabin, a further reminder of what she had lost.

∼

"There's something I need to tell you," Isobel said when she and Vic had cleared away the dinner dishes that evening. She sat on the couch to face him, deliberately making eye contact.

"I've decided to defer vet school for a year."

Vic's eyebrows shot upward.

"I'm going to New Zealand instead."

"What?" he said, like a rifle shot.

"I'm going to postpone vet school for a year and go to New Zealand to see my parents instead." She spoke the words slowly and deliberately.

Vic looked stunned. "I don't understand," he said, shaking his head.

"I want to find out who I really am."

On the verge of tears, she held her breath waiting for him to say something, but he just continued to look at her.

"Maggie gave me the money for the trip," she finally admitted.

"You told me she left you money for vet school. Are you telling me you're going to use *that*? You don't even have that money yet. It's still in escrow until probate is granted."

"No, not that money. Maggie gave me some more money, separate from the fees…another twenty-five thousand."

His mouth settled into a thin line of disapproval.

"It was all in her letter. She transferred the money into my bank account a day or two before she died. She said she knew how much it meant to me to find out who my real parents are. She wanted me to do this."

Isobel swallowed hard, trying to relieve the strangled feeling in her throat. Tears welled up in her eyes.

"Look. The only way is to go to New Zealand and talk with my…my adoptive parents."

"But why now? You could wait until Christmas and go then."

"I want to go *now*. Who knows what might happen between now and Christmas?"

"If your parents are alive now, they'll surely be there at Christmas. When did you last hear from them?"

"I got a Christmas card last year. Mom mentioned that Dad's health wasn't so good."

"And since then?"

"Nothing. I tried calling a couple of times but nobody picked up. I emailed a few times too, but again got no response.

That's pretty much the way it's been since they left Toronto. Just cards for my birthday and Christmas."

"Do you even know if they're still at the same address? They were running a bed-and-breakfast, weren't they?"

Isobel tried to suppress the anger that had begun to well up inside her. This was a side of Vic she both loved and hated, the reasonable, calm, and practical man who gave her such a sense of security. But sometimes she just wanted him to say nothing, offer no solutions, wrap his arms around her, and try to understand her misery.

"Look. I've just started to work this out. I don't know if they're still at the bed-and-breakfast." She glared at him. "Whatever. I'm going to find them and make them tell me who my real parents are. It's my last chance."

"Well, I think it's a dumb idea," Vic said, folding his arms. "If Maggie were here, she'd tell you to get on with your life, go to vet school, and wait until summer to go to New Zealand."

"No, Vic. That's what *you* are telling me. I think Maggie would say go now. Don't leave it until it's too late."

Isobel stared at him, trying to see the man she had fallen in love with. Just like everyone else, he had no idea what it felt like to be abandoned. Maggie had understood, though. She had lived with the guilt of being the offender for fifty years.

CHAPTER 5

Three weeks later, instead of attending a vet school lecture on the anatomy of the dog, Isobel left for New Zealand. Those weeks had been extraordinarily stressful — a mixture of excitement and apprehension. Vic had been withdrawn, offering her little support. With Maggie's money, she had bought a round-trip ticket from Chicago to Auckland with a return in six weeks that could be changed without penalty. The airfare had been a shock, nearly four thousand dollars. Still, there was plenty of money left for a rental car, accommodation and meals, and an international cell phone plan. She had offered to put Oliver into a kennel, but Vic wouldn't hear of it.

"No way" was his initial response followed by, "He's my hostage!"

The last address she had for her parents was a bed-and-breakfast near a town called Whitianga, three hours east of Auckland on the Coromandel Peninsula. The place still had an active website, which was reassuring. Isobel debated alerting them to her plans, but she was afraid they might tell her not to come. And then what? She would have given up her place in vet school for nothing. Pushing that thought aside, she decided she would turn up on their doorstep unannounced.

When she finally boarded the bus that would take her to O'Hare International Airport, she found herself close to tears. She and Vic had barely exchanged a word on the forty-minute drive to the bus terminal. He took her wheeled duffel from the truck and gave it to the driver while she gathered up her backpack and purse. Even with his back turned to her, she could feel his emotions. Hurt and worry mingled with resentment. He came over to where she stood on the curb, cradled her face in his hands, and looked into her eyes as if searching for reassurance.

"You'll come back, won't you?" he asked, his voice breaking. "I don't want to lose you.... I couldn't bear it."

"Don't be silly," she said, kissing him on the lips. "My two favorite things are here: you and Oliver. I promise I'll be back soon."

"I know New Zealand is nineteen hours ahead but send me an email as soon as you get to Auckland. Once you know what's going on, we can work out a regular time to talk to each other. I just want to know how you are. I wish I could go with you, but I just can't up and leave." He gave a shrug.

The night before, as they were lying together in bed, he had broken down, something Isobel had not expected. She had only seen him cry once before — the evening he learned Maggie was gone. Vic held her in silence, while she tried to push aside the guilt she felt. Then his hands began to explore her body, albeit tentatively. She ignored his unasked question and lay still, unable to quiet the maelstrom in her head. It would be weeks before she saw him again. She considered telling him she was tired, but there were already too many lies between them. She breathed deeply and shifted her hips under his caress. It was the sign he was looking for. They made love, and for a little while Isobel let her mind go blank, giving in to pleasure. Vic fell asleep soon afterwards, and she listened to his rhythmic breathing with envy. For the next several hours she lay awake, a single thought drumming through her brain. Had she made the right decision?

∼

For the last thirty minutes of the flight, all Isobel could see out her window was blue sky merging into vast ocean. This was her first time away from the North American continent. Behind her lay almost thirty years of careful planning, whereas ahead lay a vast unknown. She looked at her watch and did a rough calculation; Vic would be getting up right now and letting Oliver out. She pictured his face, his rumpled hair, the shape of his body, the familiar sounds of their morning routine. For a moment she imagined the look of loneliness in his eyes as he glanced towards her side of the bed. Quickly, she readjusted her thoughts. *She* was the one who was alone. She was about to land in a strange country where, if anything went wrong, there would be no one she could rely on to help her.

Her heart raced, and her palms grew sweaty. Closing her eyes, she slowed her breath to suppress the rising panic. She had turned her back on vet school, left Vic, abandoned Oliver, and flown halfway around the world on the chance that she could persuade her parents to tell her who she really was. Panic was replaced by anger. They knew. They had admitted as much years earlier, and yet they had refused to tell her.

"Are you all right?"

The voice came from the seat beside her. She opened her eyes and turned to look at the woman seated on her left.

A pair of bright green eyes accentuated by carefully applied black eyeliner and mascara met hers. The woman looked fresh and clean and, as far as Isobel could make out, was wearing a different outfit from when they had departed Chicago. Beside her, Isobel felt disheveled. Her crumpled shirt smelled slightly, and there was a stain on her jeans where she had spilled salad dressing when trying to open the single-serve packet.

"I'm fine," she replied, giving the woman a perfunctory smile.

She sensed the woman was trying to distract her when she pointed out the window at the first sight of land.

"We're just coming over Waiheke Island. If you look down to your right, you'll see the harbor," the woman said in a cheerful voice.

If Isobel had any doubts as to whether the woman was from New Zealand, her clipped accent and the way she said "harbor" dispelled it. She gave the woman a warmer smile and obediently peered out the window. A cluster of huge cranes hugged the shoreline, one of which arched over a cargo ship, its horizontal arm withdrawing a shipping container from the deck. Small ferry boats plied back and forth across the harbor, contrasting with a gigantic cruise ship that lay at anchor alongside the city wharf. Farther out in the water, a line of tall sailboats with massive black sails carved paths in the bay, their masts angled aggressively to catch the wind. The woman said something about the America's Cup, but Isobel wasn't listening; instead, she was mesmerized by the scene unfolding below her.

"Is this your first time to New Zealand?" the woman asked when they were taxiing to the terminal.

Isobel nodded.

"Well then, *Kia Ora*. That's the Maori greeting we use here.

It means hello or welcome, or even goodbye." She smiled. "Are you here on vacation?"

"Sort of," Isobel replied. "My parents live here."

"Oh. You're a New Zealander. I thought you were American. Sorry about that."

"Actually, I'm Canadian," Isobel replied quickly, a tiny note of resentment in her voice. Even though she was traveling on a US passport, she felt a compulsion to identify with her past in Toronto. "My mom is from New Zealand, though. She moved back here a few years ago with my dad."

Isobel realized she didn't want to talk about why she had come to New Zealand, especially not with a stranger. She smiled again, this time with the practiced skill of a school counselor dismissing a parent after an awkward conversation about their child, and turned to gather her backpack.

"I hope you have a lovely time here with your family," the woman said a few minutes later, just before their paths diverged.

A sense of purpose carried her through the formalities of Customs and Immigration, baggage claim, and picking up the keys to her rental car. Stepping outside the terminal, she sniffed at the air. It was different from Chicago, fresher and with a tang of something unfamiliar. Salt perhaps? She took a deep breath and deliberately relaxed her shoulders. There was no going back now, and no matter what she discovered, her life was going to be different. Wisconsin seemed so far away and the ties to it fragile.

"Okay, Maggie," she said under her breath as she walked to the rental car lot. "This is all your doing, so you'd better be looking out for me."

A large sign on the dashboard of the rental car reminded her to "Drive on Your Left." She plugged in the address of the airport hotel she had pre-booked, knowing a combination of jet lag and fatigue would take over once she arrived. Despite the warning, she found it surprisingly challenging to drive on the left and negotiate two roundabouts on the short drive to the hotel. At the first of the roundabouts, she had begun to turn right to merge with traffic, only to discover a car approaching from that direction. Narrowly avoiding a collision, she followed the car to her left and proceeded onwards, vowing to be more alert the next time.

Her accommodations looked like every airport chain hotel she'd encountered, impersonal and bland, but the young man at reception was efficient, and within a few minutes, she had her room key. Although she had planned to call Vic, her phone informed her it was one p.m. in Wisconsin. He would be at the job site on Lake Wisconsin where he was building a ranch-style home for a demanding client. Cell phone reception was spotty there, so she opened her email and typed, "Everything fine here in Auckland. Miss you already. Pet Oliver for me." Vic wasn't in the habit of texting, as he generally wore heavy leather gloves at work sites. She pulled the drapes and climbed into the queen-sized bed, unaccustomed to having so much space to herself. It took a while for her mind to quiet down, but eventually she fell into a deep sleep.

Chapter 6

According to Google, Whitianga was a three-hour drive from the airport. There were plenty of photos of the bed-and-breakfast on the website, together with a map, so she was confident she would find the place easily enough. Her parents would assume she was a guest when her rental car parked at the main entrance. One of them would open the front door with a practiced smile, ready to extend a welcome. But instead of the expected guest, it would be the daughter they hadn't seen in seven years.

A lump of sadness solidified in her belly when she thought back to an August in Canada a few years ago. She'd flown home to Toronto at the end of spring semester, feeling pleased at how well she had coped during her first year at the University of Wisconsin. It hadn't been easy. Despite being well mentored as a student athlete, she knew no one in Madison and found it hard to fit in. There were nights when, had she not shared her dorm room with another girl, she would have cried herself to sleep. Still, over the course of that year she had managed to maintain a 4.0 GPA and surprised herself by taking home a trophy from the All-American Invitational Tennis Tournament. With her new status as a university athlete, she had landed a paying summer job at the Aviva Stadium in Toronto where the Rogers Cup was to be held and where she would get to watch all the major players on the world tennis circuit. It had been the best summer of her life.

Coming home from the stadium one evening, Isobel was stunned when her parents told her they were emigrating to New Zealand.

Her father was the one to break the news.

"We didn't want to say anything until the summer was over, didn't want to spoil it for you."

As he spoke, his gaze shifted to the wall above her head, as if to avoid direct eye contact.

"But why? Why do you want to leave Toronto?"

Her mother answered quickly. "We never planned to stay here forever. We've been thinking about retiring to New Zealand for a long time."

"You never told me that," Isobel snapped back.

"When are you planning to leave?" she shouted at her father, forcing him to meet her gaze. "And what about me? Where am I meant to go?" The questions tumbled out. "And what about Christmas? I told you I was coming back here for Christmas. Remember?"

She looked from her father to her mother, waiting for their acknowledgment.

"Well, we're selling the house as soon as you go back to college," her mother replied with a shrug of her shoulders. "You'll just have to make your own arrangements. I suppose you could stay in Madison for Christmas — stay at your dorm, I mean."

Isobel calculated furiously. The Christmas break was

barely three weeks, too brief to make it worthwhile to fly to New Zealand. But she would have two months of vacation in summer.

"What about summer? My dorm closes in summer. Can I come to New Zealand?"

Her mother glanced briefly at her father. His face had a pained expression, his lips drawn in tightly. Again, he avoided looking at her.

"Your father and I talked about this," Isobel's mother continued. "We can't afford to bring you to New Zealand. The airfares are astronomical, and the move is already costing us a packet. You'll just have to find a job for the summer. It's probably best if you stay in Madison, easier for you to find a cheap place to stay, not like Toronto. You've got your scholarship, so you'll be all right after that."

"What about my stuff?"

"We're not planning to take much with us when we go. Shipping costs are ridiculously expensive. You should take everything you want to keep when you go back to Madison next week. Anything you leave behind..." Her mother shrugged, not finishing the sentence.

Isobel swallowed back tears. So this was it. The tenuous strings that had bound her to these two people for the past nineteen years were being unraveled. She turned abruptly and left the room.

Upstairs in her bedroom, she looked around the cramped space. Her tennis trophies dominated the room: three shelves of cups, medals, and pennants. For a brief moment she thought about packing all of them into a suitcase and taking them to Madison. There would be an excess baggage fee, no doubt. She had saved most of her earnings from summer, but even with that parsimony, she didn't have much excess cash. The reality of her new life was gradually dawning. There would be no safety net in Canada, or anywhere else. Neither of her parents had relatives in North America, which meant she had absolutely nobody to turn to if she ran out of money. From now on she would need to justify every cent.

The shelves filled with tennis trophies brought back memories of the better times in her childhood. Those trophies were witness to her determination and skill, her dedication and sacrifice, qualities her mother never seemed to notice. The elation of winning and the disappointment of second place were there on show, a reminder that she could succeed on her own. Reluctantly, she decided the trophies would have to stay behind, and indeed, most of her belongings. Besides the trophies there were childhood stuffed toys, a few framed photographs, her old Sony Walkman, some CDs, a few books, and a box of "treasures." Not much to show for nineteen years of life. Still, she desperately wanted to take something to remember her childhood. She decided to take the treasure box. Cracking open the lid, she dropped in one of her tennis medals, before closing it firmly.

Even though her job at the tennis stadium was officially over, for the remaining week of her vacation Isobel went there each day. She couldn't bear to be around her parents who, now that they had told her their plans, felt free to get on with the business of selling their house. Cardboard moving boxes appeared in the garage, waiting to be filled.

~

Her father drove her to the airport. She and her mother had exchanged perfunctory hugs before Isobel climbed into the car, and as she left the familiar tree-lined street for the last time, she didn't look back. At Toronto Pearson Airport her father had taken her suitcase from the trunk and placed it on the curb while she gathered her backpack and coat. He had never been an affectionate man, so his hug was a surprise. She wished there had been more of them. Those hugs would have acknowledged how hard she worked at school to make him proud of her. They would have softened the disappointment of tennis matches lost. Above all, they would have reassured her that even if her mother was cold and distant, he at least had a place in his heart for her.

"Here's something for you," he said, handing her an envelope. "It's not a lot."

He turned to leave but seemed to think the better of it. His final words stayed with her for a long time afterwards.

"We did the best we could."

Later, when the Air Canada pilot announced that they had crossed the Canadian border, Isobel opened the envelope. It contained a thousand American dollars. She closed her eyes and allowed the accumulated misery of the past week to wash over her.

Chapter 7

Her mind had been on what she was going to say to her parents when she exited the hotel parking lot the following morning into the wrong lane of traffic. A truck barreled towards her, honking its horn furiously, and she swerved to the left. It raced by, passing within inches of her front bumper. Abruptly, she pulled over to the side of the road and waited for her hands to stop shaking before continuing on her way in the left lane, listening attentively to the phone's verbal instructions. She dared not take her eyes off the road.

The Coromandel Peninsula was touted by tourist websites as one of the loveliest places in North Island. The remoteness of it seemed at odds with her parents' lifestyle. She had always thought of them as city people, comfortable in the densely packed inner suburbs of Toronto. In contrast, the nearest town to their bed-and-breakfast was easily twenty miles to the south, according to the Google route map, and accessed by a narrow, winding, hilly road that ended at the tip of the peninsula. She gave the road her full attention. For several miles tall trees bordered it, eclipsing any view, so it came as a relief when the road straightened out and descended into open farmland where cattle and sheep grazed.

As she rounded a right-angled corner, the ocean finally came into view. To her right stretched a vast sweep of shoreline with perfect white sands. She drove along the coast for a couple of miles until, gradually, signs of civilization appeared: small white houses with metal roofs; a paved path paralleling the road on the ocean side; a sign indicating fire danger, its arrow pointed reassuringly into the green zone. A hillside rose to her left, barren except for patches of reed grass with white bushy tips swaying in the onshore breeze. Even as she scanned the road for the entrance to the bed-and-breakfast, she managed to miss it. Turning around at a public campground a few hundred yards farther up the road, she drove back the way she had come, slower this time. A small oval sign, partially hidden in shrubbery adjacent to a narrow driveway, announced "Kuaotunu Bay Lodge." Her heart began to race as she turned the car into the entrance and drove up a steep hill to a group of buildings that faced the ocean.

The lodge consisted of a long rectangular building with a deep veranda sheltered by an overhanging roof. A smaller second story with its own small balcony was partially inset into the center of the building. Unlike many houses she had seen thus far, the roof was shingled with sandy brown tiles that blended perfectly with the lodge's brick walls. All the doors and windows were open, their turquoise frames highlighting the roof gutters, which were painted the same bright color. A little farther up the hillside stood another smaller structure with the same color scheme, its roof line and tiny veranda matching that of the lodge. Lush flowering shrubs bordered the veranda, ending at a lawn that stretched downward towards the sea. Out of the corner of her eye, Isobel caught sight of a wrought iron table and two chairs on the lawn positioned perfectly to take advantage of the stunning view. The lodge exuded a quiet comfort.

Over the past two days she had rehearsed what she would say when she finally saw her parents, modifying the words and the tone innumerable times. "Hi. I was in the area" sounded ridiculous, as did "I thought I'd surprise you." One part of her wanted to scream at them, giving voice to the pent-up rage and frustration of the previous years. But on this final leg of the journey, she had come to the reluctant conclusion the best approach was to say nothing and wait until one of them spoke. Let them set the tone and then decide.

She parked the rental car, walked to the front door, and taking a deep breath, pushed the buzzer. From somewhere inside the house, a ringing tone echoed, followed a minute later by footsteps. The door opened, and an unfamiliar face looked at her questioningly.

"Hello," the woman said. "You must be Sally. We weren't expecting you until tomorrow." She opened the door wide to allow Isobel to come inside.

"I'm sorry," Isobel stuttered. "I'm...actually, I wasn't expected. I'm looking for the Babićs. Christina and Novak." Her voice trailed away.

"Oh." The woman sounded surprised. "They don't live here anymore. Not for two years now."

Isobel put her hand to her chest, her mouth agape.

Seeing her dismay, the woman said, "Why don't you come in, dear?"

She closed the door behind Isobel and led her into a spacious living room that was flooded with light. A breeze drifted in through the open patio doors.

"They moved to South Island. Why don't you have a seat,

and I'll go look for their address." She gestured to a sofa. "It's somewhere in the office. I think I remember where I put it."

The woman's footsteps echoed down a corridor, followed by the sound of drawers being opened and a rustle of papers. This continued for several minutes while Isobel waited, indifferent to the view. Her predicament elicited a grim smile. Maggie might have set this plan in motion, but she was also the person who had cautioned Isobel in one of their heart-to-heart conversations, "Always have a back-up plan."

She stood up when she heard footsteps approaching. The woman returned with a triumphant smile on her face, waving a piece of paper.

"Here we are. There's no telephone number or email or anything. Looks like they moved to a place called Motueka. It's a small town on South Island. Somewhere near Nelson, I think."

Seeing Isobel's puzzled look, she added, "Nelson is on the north of the island. It's quite a ways from here, though, if you were thinking of driving, that is. You'd have to take a ferry."

Isobel sank back down on the sofa. She gave a weak smile.

"I was in Auckland on a business trip, you see, and thought I'd surprise them. I checked the website and just assumed they were still running the bed-and-breakfast. I never considered they had moved. I got a card from them last Christmas." She gave a sigh. "I should have checked. It was stupid of me."

The woman gave her a sympathetic look.

"It would be such a pity to have come all this way and not get to see them. Are they good friends of yours?"

Isobel had anticipated this question while she was waiting for the woman to find her parents' new address and was ready with an answer.

"My aunt and uncle. I haven't seen them since they moved here from Toronto several years ago."

"That sounds about right. They told us when we bought the bed-and-breakfast that they had been here for five years or so. I think it must have gotten to be too much for them in the end. His health wasn't so good, you know." She tut-tutted sympathetically.

Isobel stood to leave, then paused.

"The sign down by the road said 'Vacancy.' Would it be possible for me to stay here tonight? I'm still a bit jet-lagged, and the drive from Auckland was exhausting. I cannot imagine driving back there in the dark."

"Oh, I totally understand. We do have a vacancy. Only one other room is occupied right now — a nice German couple. We'll be full tomorrow night, though, so you'd have to leave by noon. Would that be all right?"

Although it was only midafternoon, Isobel felt as if she had climbed a mountain only to discover the actual peak was still far in the distance.

"That would be wonderful," she said, sighing with relief. "Thank you so much."

The woman introduced herself as Marjorie and showed Isobel to a room at the end of a corridor. Picture windows looked out on the bay where crystal blue water shimmered in the afternoon light.

"There's coffee and tea things on top of the fridge, and I'll bring a couple of slices of my homemade cake in a few minutes. Breakfast is at eight-thirty in the dining room. You'll probably meet the German couple at breakfast. They're very nice, and they speak perfect English."

Marjorie pointed to a folder on a desk by the bed. "The Wi-Fi password is in there, together with a lot of information about what's to see in the area. But I know you'll be leaving tomorrow." She paused to catch her breath. "At any rate, if you need anything, just come to the living room and call out if we're not around. My husband will be back soon. Ray. He grew up on South Island, so he'll be able to tell you a lot more about Motueka."

~

It was too chilly to sit at the bistro table on the tiny patio outside her room, so Isobel took a seat by the window instead, a mug of coffee in her hand, and stared out at the ocean. The bay was bracketed by two headlands and in between, in the far distance, she could make out the hint of an island. Her thoughts returned to her parents and how she might get to Motueka. She opened her computer and tapped the name into Google Search. The drive south to the ferry terminal would take approximately fifteen hours. According to the timetable, ferries departed every couple of hours, although passengers were warned to book in advance to be assured a passage. She calculated that if she left Kuaotunu early the following morning, she could be in Motueka the day after. The only alternative was to drive back to Auckland, return her rental car, and fly to Nelson. Another search showed that Air New Zealand had several flights from Auckland to Nelson each day.

A growl from her stomach reminded her that, except for the coffee and two slices of fruitcake Marjorie had delivered, she hadn't eaten all day. She tried to remember whether she had seen any restaurants on the winding road from Whitianga, the last town she had driven through. None came to mind.

She went to the living room and called out, "Anyone home?"

A man's voice replied, "Coming," and soon afterwards a rotund, red-faced, smiling man appeared in the doorway. He introduced himself as Ray, Marjorie's husband.

"You're the young lady from Canada who's looking for your auntie and uncle. I'm sorry that you had to come all the way here to find out…well, to find Marjorie and me. Hah! We're glad you're with us now, though. What can I do for you?"

Isobel liked Ray immediately.

"I was wondering if you could tell me where I might get some dinner. It doesn't have to be fancy. I just don't want to drive back to Whitianga, if possible."

"You must be exhausted after the drive from Auckland, and you only arrived in the country a few days ago. Yes? Well, all we can offer you is Luke's, Luke's Kitchen to be precise. Actually, the food is pretty good. He does a great pizza, and you're in luck, 'cause he's open tonight. Pity though. It's too early in the season for the live music." His frown was replaced by a sunny smile. "It's about a mile back the way you came, just off the main road. You could walk there if you were feeling up to it. There's a footpath the whole way." The frown returned as he glanced out the window. "Mind you, it would be dark by the time you got back. Still, I could give you a flashlight." Noticing Isobel's raised eyebrows, he added, "Trust me, it's completely safe. No worries there." Seeing her indecision, he added, "I'll leave the flashlight outside your door in case you change your mind."

She thanked him and returned to her room. Rather than working out whether it was day or night in Wisconsin at this moment or where Vic might be, she typed a quick email describing what had happened. The thought of talking with him now, of trying to sound upbeat and confident, was dispiriting. She was afraid she might break down and cry if she heard his voice.

Luke's Kitchen was a welcome sight after a twenty-minute brisk walk along the footpath that paralleled the shore. The restaurant had charm, with enough funkiness to make even the most discriminating diner feel at ease. About half of the tables were occupied, and a steady buzz of conversation filled the air, punctuated by the occasional burst of laughter. Isobel walked through the main dining area and took a seat at the bar. She had planned to order the wood-fired pizza, but the night's special, scrawled on a sandwich board at the entrance, sounded intriguing: "Fresh fish curry that comes with a glass of Koparepare Chardonnay. Koparepare donates a portion of sales to the nonprofit LegaSea. Do some good, drink some good!"

The barman turned from chatting with one of the waitresses. "What can I get you?" he asked Isobel, giving her his full attention.

She guessed he was about thirty, with dark hair, a scruffy beard, and eyes that smiled mischievously. He was wearing a black baseball cap with the restaurant logo on it and a plain white T-shirt. Despite her hunger and fatigue, she found herself wanting to engage in conversation, if only to distract herself from the day's disappointments.

"How can I resist ordering the special if I'm going to save the world at the same time?" she said, returning his smile.

He laughed, and she noticed that one of his front teeth was chipped, giving him a rakish appearance.

"Are you here on vacation?" he asked. Isobel heard the hint of an American accent.

"Sort of. I was planning to visit my aunt and uncle at the bed-and-breakfast up the road, but it seems they sold it a couple of years ago and moved to South Island. I'm staying there tonight. I'll head back to Auckland in the morning."

"Seems a shame to have come all this way for nothing. Still, I promise you the food won't disappoint, and the wine is great. Plus, you'll be saving the world." He grinned again.

"Are you from the US?" she asked.

"Nah. Canada, actually."

"Really. Me too, though I live in the States now. Where in Canada?"

"British Columbia, north of Vancouver, near Squamish." He gave a shrug. "I decided to take a break and check out the rest of the world. Hard to believe it but I've been here a year already. I really like this place." He gave her a lopsided grin. "They don't let you stay forever, though, so I'll probably go back to Canada in a year or so."

The sound of a bell tinkling caught his attention, and he looked in the direction of the kitchen. A young woman was beckoning him.

"Oops. Gotta go. My name's Paul, by the way. If I get a chance, I'll come back and chat some more. If you're staying around for a few days, we do a great breakfast here too."

He disappeared into the kitchen, and his place was taken at the bar by the young woman who had waved to him. Isobel's meal arrived, and she was glad she had chosen the special. The curry was unlike anything she had tasted before — tender pieces of flaky fish in a coconut milk broth with a hint of coriander and something else that she subsequently learned was curry leaves. The wine was excellent too.

"Can I get you another glass?" the young woman asked. But Isobel declined, thinking of the walk back to the bed-and-breakfast in the dark, even with the help of a flashlight.

An elderly couple approached her.

"Are you Isobel?" the man asked. It sounded as if he had inserted extra 'z's into the middle of her name and added another 'l' at the end. Izzobelle.

Before she could answer, his companion chimed in.

"We are also staying at the bed-and-breakfast. Marjorie said that you had walked here and might like to drive back to the house with us. But perhaps you want to stay longer?"

Isobel would have liked to stay, sip another glass of wine, perhaps chat some more with Paul, but the prospect of being in her bed within ten minutes was too appealing.

"Thank you so much. I'd love a ride back. Just let me pay and I'll be ready to leave."

On the short drive back to the lodge, Isobel couldn't help noticing how successfully the woman negotiated driving on the left. She consoled herself when she learned the couple had been staying at the bed-and-breakfast for a week, using it as a base from which to explore the area. While she still hadn't made up her mind about how to get to South Island, the prospect of driving for fifteen hours through the length of North Island on the wrong side of the road was daunting. The decision could wait; she would make up her mind in the morning. For now, all she wanted was to go to bed and sleep.

Chapter 8

At breakfast the following morning, Isobel was joined by the German couple, who were disappointed to learn she was returning to Auckland.

"There is so much to see here in the Coromandel, and it is so beautiful. We too are leaving today, but not to the city. Instead, we go to Rotorua to see the Maori village."

"And the geysers," his wife added.

He patted his stomach. "We will miss Marjorie's breakfasts. She makes her own peach preserves from the trees behind the house."

Even after a good night's sleep, the prospect of driving to South Island was unsettling; New Zealand highways fell far short of their American counterparts. Isobel's new plan was to drive back to the airport in Auckland, stay overnight at the same hotel, and fly to Nelson the following morning. Her arrival time would be the same as if she drove, and this way she could relax a little, perhaps even see a bit of the Coromandel. Before breakfast she had booked a flight, the disappointment of the previous day replaced by optimism. Internal flights were surprisingly expensive, and she was beginning to accept that the entire trip might well end up costing twenty-five thousand dollars. For some reason this made her feel better about her lie to Vic about how much money Maggie had given her.

"What was your favorite beach in this area?" she asked the German couple. "I'd love to go for a walk on a beach before I head back to the city."

The couple talked briefly in German, their nodding heads indicating a consensus.

"Otama Beach," they answered in unison. "It is close to here. You go to Luke's and drive over the hill. The road is very winding and narrow, and it is made of...gravel, but it is good."

His wife butted in. "There are many places to pull over and look at the view."

He continued. "The road ends at Otama Beach. And you can go to Luke's for kaffee and kuchen afterwards. No?"

Soon Isobel said her goodbyes to Marjorie and Ray, thanked them for their kindness, and complimented Marjorie on the breakfast.

"I hope you find your auntie and uncle, dear," she said with genuine concern in her voice. "Tell them we love this place and are so grateful they sold it to us."

∼

The parking lot at Luke's was easily half full when she turned the corner — the breakfast crowd, no doubt. She continued uphill, the road narrowing and blacktop giving way to gravel. Each turn revealed even more spectacular views. Pulling off the road at the highest point, she glanced at her cell phone. It showed five bars. She did a quick calculation and realized that Vic might be at home right now as it was the weekend. She dialed the landline; cell service was notoriously unreliable in the valley. Giddy with anticipation, she listened to the familiar ringtone, expecting to hear his cheery voice. Instead, her own voice came on the line, asking the caller to leave a message.

"Hi. It's me. I thought I might catch you. Just to let you know I'm going to fly to Nelson tomorrow morning. I'm driving back to Auckland right now." She paused, at a loss as to what else to say. "I'll try to call you tomorrow. Love you."

Fifteen minutes later, a weather-worn sign beside a small parking lot showed she had arrived at Otama Beach. The breeze carried a chill, and she pulled on a jacket. Happy to be able to stretch her legs, she set out. Besides the walk to the restaurant the previous evening, the last time she had taken a walk was several days ago, her regular evening walk with Oliver around the perimeter of the prairie. The comparison could not have been more striking. A sweeping arc of silvery gray beach stretched in front of her, empty except for the occasional shore-bird playing in the froth of the receding waves. For a while she stood, staring at a piece of driftwood trapped at the shoreline. Where had it come from? She tried to picture a globe but wasn't sure what other land masses were at the same latitude as this remote peninsula. A wave of loneliness swept over her, and she quickened her pace, focusing on the headland at the end of the bay where she would turn around and retrace her steps.

By the time she got back to the car, she was looking forward to warming up with a cup of coffee and a pastry at Luke's Kitchen. Her thoughts drifted back to the previous evening and the young Canadian, Paul. They were about the same age, yet their lives had taken very different directions. Hers had been a linear trajectory from high school to college, to a secure job. That desire for stability and security had guided her life up to a year ago when she realized how unhappy she had become. Pursuing a career in veterinary medicine had offered a lifeline. And now she had thrown that away.

Less than half the tables in the restaurant were occupied. Isobel chose one near the bar, sat down, and looked around, but there was no sign of Paul. An unfamiliar waitress appeared and took her order for coffee and a slice of homemade quiche. She would have liked a glass of wine, but the drive back to Auckland on winding narrow roads intimidated her. She looked at her watch. There was still plenty of time before it got dark. She lingered for another hour, checked her watch again, then asked for the bill. Reluctantly, she set out for Auckland.

Chapter 9

For much of the ninety-minute flight they had been in the clouds, leaving Isobel with little to distract her from her thoughts. What if her parents didn't want to talk to her? She imagined a scenario where she was standing on their doorstep, begging them to let her inside, pleading with them to answer her questions. For a moment she felt as if she were suffocating. Tightening her hands into fists, she closed her eyes and began to take deliberately slow breaths. The panic receded gradually, and by the time the plane touched down, she was in control again.

She had decided to drive straight to Motueka, barely an hour northwest of Nelson Airport. At the outskirts of the city, she noticed a sign on the side of the road for "The Ruby Coast Scenic Route." The two-lane road meandered north past commercial apple and kiwi orchards and vineyards, and while it was still early spring, it felt much warmer than the Coromandel, despite being several hundred miles closer to Antarctica.

Finally, she saw a sign for Motueka. A glance at her phone indicated she was ten minutes from her destination. Her mouth felt dry, and she licked her lips to moisten them. A McDonalds with its characteristic golden arches momentarily distracted her, and she almost missed the right turn into Kotara Street. Here the houses were all single story, some with fences and neat lawns. Each house had a flat metal mailbox by the entrance with a number displayed on it. She drove slowly, glancing at the numbers as they increased, odds on the right, evens on the left. It must be garbage collection day, she thought, for each house had a large black wheeled bin with an orange lid at the curb, together with a smaller blue bin, perhaps for recycling. The line of houses on the left ended abruptly, and for a moment she thought Marjorie must have made a mistake, as she could see a T-junction ahead that marked the end of the street.

Number sixty-three was the second last house on the right — a neat modern bungalow with a well-tended lawn. The gate across the driveway was open, but for some reason she couldn't quite explain, Isobel didn't want to turn into the driveway. Instead, she drove past the house, made a U-turn at the junction, and returned to park on the street just out of sight of the house.

She took a deep breath and walked up the driveway to the front door, wondering if anyone had noticed her, or indeed, whether her parents would recognize her. Her appearance hadn't changed much, and her weight was the same as when she left Canada. But she had let her hair grow since giving up competitive tennis, and she no longer dressed like a student. Seven years since she had last seen them. Almost a quarter of her life. Her heart was pounding.

She rang the bell. A few moments later she heard the approaching sound of shoes on a hard surface.

"Coming…"

It was her mother's voice.

The door opened.

"Hi, Mom."

She watched as her mother's face registered a series of emotions, ranging from shock to recognition to incredulity.

"Isobel! Where...? How...?" Her mouth was slightly open as she shook her head slowly from side to side. "I don't believe it," she gasped.

Isobel was shocked to see how much older her mother looked. She had let her hair go gray, and deep lines were etched around her mouth. Since their relationship had never been an affectionate one, Isobel was taken aback when her mother put her arms out to give her a hug. She stepped forward awkwardly and allowed herself to be embraced, her body taut with mistrust.

"Come in. Come in. Your father will be so pleased to see you."

The words spilled out, and for the first time, Isobel noticed her mother's New Zealand accent. She stepped into a wide hallway and followed her mother into what was clearly the sitting room. It was a bright, airy space, with large square windows that looked out towards the street. Her mother turned to face her, hands upturned, a questioning look on her face.

"Where's your car? I didn't hear you drive up."

Isobel gestured to the street where the rear bumper of her rental car was just visible through the window.

"I parked it on the street, just in case I got the wrong house." She shrugged. "I didn't know if you would still be living at this address. Marjorie said it's been two years since she spoke to you, so..."

"You saw Marjorie?"

"Well, yeah. I thought you and Dad were still running the bed-and-breakfast, so I went there first. That's the last address

I had for you." She tried not to sound aggrieved. "Marjorie was really nice. I stayed there a night. It's a beautiful place."

"Let me get your father," her mother said, turning abruptly as if to leave the room. She stopped and came back to where Isobel was standing.

"He's not well. I'm just warning you ahead of time.... You'll be shocked when you see him."

While she waited, Isobel looked around the comfortable space, recognizing a few pieces of furniture from their sitting room in Toronto. A framed photograph, strategically positioned to hide a water stain, stood on a familiar mahogany side table. With a flash of recognition, Isobel remembered that it was she who had been responsible for that stain, a nine-year old's mistake of over-watering a plant that had once stood there. She glanced at the photograph and was astonished to see it was of her and her parents, taken around the time of her high school graduation.

"Look who's come to see us."

Her mother's cheery voice emerged from the back of the house. Isobel turned abruptly and felt the blood rising into her cheeks as if she had been caught doing something untoward. Her mother was pushing a wheelchair in which a small, balding figure sat hunched. Isobel didn't recognize her father at first. A pair of black-rimmed glasses were propped on the end of his nose, giving him an intellectual look. Two thin plastic tubes led from a small machine hanging off the side of the wheelchair, to loop over his ears and end just below his nostrils. Her mother positioned the wheelchair to look out towards the garden and set the brake. She plugged in the machine, which began to make a series of popping noises before settling into a steady low hum. For a moment nobody said anything. Then Isobel went over to her father, squatting down in front of him, and took his hands in hers.

"Hi, Dad. It's Isobel."

He raised his head and looked at her, but the eyes in the upturned face were vacant. She looked towards her mother.

"You'll have to speak up. He's quite deaf without his hearing aids." She pursed her lips. "He hates wearing them."

Isobel tried again, and this time he seemed to recognize her. She could feel a tentative pressure on her fingers.

"Isobel," he said and smiled.

Her mother repositioned the wheelchair slightly so that he could see Isobel when she sat down on the sofa.

"I'll get us a cup of tea while you chat."

A few moments later Isobel heard the sound of a kettle being filled. Tea. Maggie used to call it a universal solvent, and during the year Isobel had spent looking after Maggie, she too had come to recognize its healing qualities.

Her father continued to stare at her, and Isobel wasn't sure what to say next.

"What sort of car did you rent?" he asked, his voice weak yet familiar.

Her father had an accent too, and Isobel wondered how it was she had never noticed before. His question seemed out of context, but then she remembered that he had always liked cars. To her mother's chagrin, he used to spend hours tinkering with whatever secondhand car the family owned at the time. No engine was immune from his desire to improve its performance. And whereas her mother would have preferred a reliable Japanese car, his curiosity tended towards more exotic Renaults and Fiats, the least suitable vehicles for a Toronto winter. As a result, Isobel had become adept at using the public transport system to travel to the tennis club. Thinking about tennis brought back bitter memories of her parents' lack of involvement in her life. She felt a stab of guilt and quickly pushed the thought from her mind.

"A Toyota Corolla," she replied, mouthing the word in an exaggerated fashion.

Her father let out a brief laugh that degenerated into a hacking cough. When it finally subsided, he looked at her intently as if to take in every feature of her face. The room was eerily quiet except for a gentle hiss coming from the oxygen machine, followed by the growingly insistent whistle of a kettle from the kitchen. Unsure what to do next, Isobel described her visit to the bed-and-breakfast, meeting Marjorie and Ray, her dinner at Luke's Kitchen, and the walk along Otuna Beach the previous day. She spoke loudly, hoping her father could hear but also her mother, who was surely listening. As a child Isobel had never understood why her mother seemed to begrudge the time her father and she spent together. But as she grew older, she began to understand the subtle dynamics within their family. Her mother seemed to resent her. If her father suggested that Isobel go with him to pick up a pizza for dinner or accompany him to the car parts store, her mother always seemed to find something else for her to do — a trivial chore that could not be postponed.

Isobel talked for a full five minutes, describing everything that had happened since she arrived in New Zealand. At times she wasn't sure if her father was still listening. His head drooped and his eyes were closed, although his eyelids fluttered occasionally as if in response to a particularly vivid or familiar memory. When she finally stopped talking, her mother reappeared with a teapot, milk jug, three mugs, and a plate of cookies.

She handed Isobel a mug saying, "A splash of milk and no sugar. See, I still remember," giving her daughter a rare smile.

With surprising tenderness, she placed a mug on her husband's lap, wrapping his fingers around the handle. When she had offered Isobel a cookie, her mother took another and carefully set it beside her husband's mug, within easy reach of his hand.

"I couldn't help hearing you telling your father about Kaoutunu Bay Lodge. We loved it there, didn't we Novak?"

Her father nodded his head slowly, then raised the mug to his lips. Satisfied that he could manage his tea, Isobel's mother turned to her.

"And the bed-and-breakfast was quite a success, especially after all the work your father put into it. It was pretty rundown when we bought it, but he was always a wizard with his hands. He re-did most of the built-ins, the kitchen cupboards, even the floors. And the bathrooms...he completely remodeled all of them. We didn't go to Luke's that often; we were too busy with getting the place in shape and after that, looking after guests."

She paused to take a sip of tea. Isobel wanted to ask why they had left, but over the course of the past half an hour, it had become painfully obvious. She wasn't sure whether her father had dementia or Parkinson's or something else. But whatever it was, there was no way they could have continued running a bed-and-breakfast.

"And then we came down here." Her mother said in an upbeat tone, and Isobel quickly responded.

"It's lovely here. I haven't seen much, but the drive from the airport was very pretty. I guess that's why they call it a scenic route. Ruby Coast. I saw the sign as I was leaving Nelson."

"It gets better as you go north. And then there's Abel Tasman, of course."

Her mother offered her another cookie, but she declined. Not sure how to break the silence, Isobel asked what she thought was an innocuous question.

"Why South Island?"

"I'm from South Island originally," her mother replied.

"I never knew that. I mean, I knew you were born in New Zealand, but I didn't know where."

"You never asked."

The rebuke hurt, but Isobel realized her mother's statement was true. As a child and later a teenager, she had never shown any interest in where her mother came from. Everyone in Toronto had a parent or grandparent born outside of Canada, so it wasn't anything special or deserving of curiosity. Besides, New Zealand had always appeared tiny on the world map, remote and unimportant.

"Where were you born?" Isobel asked tentatively.

"South of here. Almost at the tip of the island, near Invercargill. I grew up on a farm there.

"But you left...."

"Yes. The farm was in a pretty remote place. This was before the *Lord of the Rings* craze, so nobody went there. Nowadays it's on the tourist trail, like everywhere else in this country."

Isobel smiled at her mother, encouraging her to continue.

"After high school I went to nursing college in Dunedin. That's another city farther up the east coast. Once I had my nursing certification, I left. Lots of us nurses emigrated, mostly to England, though some went to Canada. We were part of the Commonwealth you see, and it was easy to move around. You didn't have to take another set of exams in Canada in those days."

She smiled, and for a moment the weariness left her face.

"I'd always wanted to see what it would be like to live in a big city, so I picked Toronto."

She shifted in her chair a little. "And now I'm back here. We are." She looked towards her husband, her features softening into a brief smile.

Isobel looked over at her father. He hadn't said anything for a long time, although he raised the mug to his lips every so often, so she knew he was awake.

"Whereabouts are you staying?" her mother asked.

Isobel didn't know what to say; she hadn't thought much beyond her arrival at her parents' house. Now, having seen their situation, she felt uncomfortable.

"I suppose I could make up a bed for you in the study," her mother continued. "We only have the two bedrooms and your father needs...space."

"No. Don't do that," Isobel said, shaking her head. "I passed several hotels on the way here. I can easily find a room."

There was a painful silence, during which Isobel realized there was no way she could ask her father the question that had been consuming her for weeks and months, if not years. Her mother took the mug from her husband and placed it back on the tray.

"It's time for your nap dear," she said and looked from her husband to Isobel. "He gets very tired before his dialysis. The best time is afterwards."

"Oh. Sure. I understand."

Isobel got up from the sofa and placed her mug back on the tray. She hesitated for a moment, looking first at her father, then her mother.

"I'd like to come back if I could — catch up some more. Would that be okay?"

"Of course," her mother said. "Tomorrow is your father's dialysis day. We'll be going to the hospital in Nelson early and won't get back here until late afternoon. You could come for dinner tomorrow evening, if you like."

"That's great. Just in case anything changes, I'll give you my cell number." She called out the digits to her mother, who wrote them down on a slip of paper.

"My email is still the same," she added, making an effort to mask the reproach she felt. "I better get your landline and cell numbers as well." She was determined not to lose her parents again.

Crossing the room to her father's wheelchair, she bent down and gave him a tentative hug. She caught sight of her mother looking at her and wondered what she was thinking. It had probably been her mother's idea to move back to New Zealand. Whether her father would have preferred to stay in Toronto, Isobel didn't know. She remembered how he would come home from work in the evenings exhausted, with barely enough energy to have a conversation over dinner with her and her mother. Life must have become increasingly challenging for her mother over the past few years, watching her husband deteriorate. Isobel felt a twinge of something unfamiliar — pity.

Chapter 10

It was barely four o'clock and Isobel felt drained, not just physically but emotionally. The shock of finding her parents had grown old clung to her like a cold, wet blanket. She felt guilty too, at not having made more of an effort to reach out to them over the past seven years. True, they hadn't risen to the challenge of long-distance communication either. Nevertheless, she could have tried harder. Like most people her age, she was comfortable with all the latest apps and communicated regularly with friends, but her parents had always been old-fashioned, preferring hand-written letters. It had taken them some time to adapt to email.

Returning to the main street in Motueka, it hardly mattered which direction she drove. She'd find a hotel, get a room for the night, and ask whoever was at the reception desk where she might eat. After all, that approach had worked at Kaoutunu. Her mind drifted back to the bed-and-breakfast, Luke's Kitchen, Otuna Beach. Had that been only yesterday? It seemed such a long time ago.

She turned north, remonstrating with herself. It had

been stupid not to do some homework before flying halfway around the world. She could easily have bought a New Zealand guidebook and brought it along with her. But during those last few weeks in Wisconsin, she had been focused on how to get to her parents' bed-and-breakfast and little else. Now, with twenty-four hours stretching ahead of her and no objective, she felt unmoored.

A blue sign with the outline of a bicycle on it caught her attention, and indeed, there was a narrow bike lane on the left side of the road. Curious as to where it led, she paid attention to subsequent blue signs and after a few miles found herself following them to a right turn off the main road. Leaving behind apple orchards and hop fields, the ocean came into view — a perfect crescent of blue water. Coming to a fork in the road, the now-familiar blue sign had an additional piece of information: Abel Tasman National Park. Putting it all together — the Ruby Coast Scenic Route, her mother mentioning Abel Tasman, the dedicated cycle path — she found herself smiling. Cycling was one of her pleasures, and the roads around where she lived in Wisconsin were particularly popular with Madison bicycle clubs. What would it be like, she wondered, to come to New Zealand on a cycling vacation? The scenery was breathtaking, and the roads relatively flat. And if Luke's Kitchen was anything to go by, there could be a great coffee shop or restaurant destination on every ride.

She continued to follow the blue signs. The road narrowed suddenly, and she slowed as she drove through a series of sharp curves. Here, road signs reminded motorists that cyclists used the same lane as they did and to give them space. A few miles farther, a camper van parked in a pull-off with a prominent for sale sign taped to the window caught her attention. The notion of being able to drive around the country in an RV, stopping anywhere to cycle or hike or swim, pulling into a campground for the night with everything one needed in the camper van struck Isobel as an idyllic vacation.

"I would love to do that," she said aloud, but the weight of her current reality bore down, quieting her imagination.

The bicycle path finally came to an end at a spacious parking lot. A few cars and camper vans were parked in such a way as to take full advantage of the view of the bay. Two small kiosks advertised their services — Abel Tasman Water Sports and Tasman Aqua Taxi. Isobel pulled in beside the last car, took out her cell phone, and scrolled through the list of nearby hotels. The name Kimi Ora Eco Resort sounded interesting, and it had a restaurant, which meant she would not have to go in search of a meal. It looked relatively close on the map, so she tapped the screen for directions. Five minutes later she turned into the entrance and drove up a winding avenue bordered by lush growth, to a building situated on a terrace overlooking the bay. The hotel had an air of luxury, and in the past Isobel would never have chosen to stay in such a place. But by now she was exhausted, and the prospect of seeking out a cheaper hotel was beyond her. Silently she paid homage to Maggie, who, even in death, was taking care of her.

Two wooden pillars festooned with intricate carvings flanked the entrance. Stepping out of the car, Isobel was struck by the smells: salt and seaweed combined with earthy tropical foliage and a hint of flowers. Birds flitted around, indifferent to her presence. She paused for a moment to listen to the reassuring rhythmic pulse of the ocean, then walked into the building.

A young, athletic-looking woman in her mid-twenties looked up from the reception desk.

"Can I help you?"

"I was wondering if you have a room free? I don't have a reservation," Isobel added hastily.

"Is it just for the one night?" the woman asked.

Isobel hesitated before answering. Even though she would be going back to her parents' house the following afternoon, she would still need somewhere to stay that night too.

"Two nights," she replied.

"We have a couple of different rooms: a studio and a one-bedroom. They both have balconies that look out on Kaiteriteri Bay, but the one-bedroom has a jacuzzi." She mentioned the price of each room, adding that breakfast was included.

It was an indulgence, but Isobel justified it by reminding herself that she had barely relaxed since leaving Wisconsin.

"The larger room, please."

With the key card in her hand, she followed the woman's directions and found herself stepping into a spacious bedroom with a king-sized bed. Immediately her eyes were drawn to the floor-to ceiling windows that comprised one wall of the room. She walked over to them and sat for a moment on the chaise that was positioned to take full advantage of the view of the bay. It was magnificent.

"Thank you, Maggie," she whispered, before getting up to open the sliding doors.

Despite the early evening chill, she stood for a few minutes on the terrace, thinking about the events of the last few weeks. Maggie's death, her decision to find her parents, forgoing vet school (and lying to Vic about it), flying to New Zealand, her disappointment at the bed-and-breakfast, and now, today, seeing her parents for the first time in years. Her father had been the biggest shock. She remembered the argument she had with Vic about not wanting to wait until summer to make the trip in case her parents might die. At the time those were just words thrown out in an argument; she had never considered they might be true.

For the first time ever, Isobel felt a growing sense of solicitude for her mother. True, she had cared for Maggie, but during that time Vic had been there to share the burden. Her mother's situation was very different. She probably didn't have many friends in Motueka, considering they had moved to the town barely two years ago. Who did she have to turn to? Back in Wisconsin when Isobel had needed help, Vic had been there. That was one of the best things about him; he loved to help people. But that was part of the problem too — he couldn't help her here, and it left him frustrated. What she needed from him now more than ever was empathy and understanding.

She closed her eyes and imagined Vic standing beside her. He would love this place. Perhaps she should have tried harder to persuade him to come along, but it wouldn't have worked. He'd have been a distraction, impatient to do something, go kayaking or hiking or fishing. No. This was something she had to do alone. Maybe in the future they would come back to New Zealand together, but it seemed unlikely. Once she got the information she wanted, she didn't ever need to see her parents again.

She looked at her watch, which showed five p.m. A check on her phone confirmed it was ten p.m. the previous evening in Chicago. It seemed so strange to be calling Vic yesterday, but she wanted to talk to him, to hear his voice. She was surprised when he didn't answer the phone. Unless the landline was damaged, he must be out. There was another possibility, of course. Once before a beaver had chewed through a willow tree near the pond that subsequently took down the telephone line. Maybe the line was down again. Disappointed, she considered her options. It was still too early for dinner, and although she felt drained, her body was still tense from sitting since early morning. She remembered the parking lot with the kayaks, barely five minutes from the hotel by car and decided to drive back there and go for a walk.

The beach was empty except for a man walking his dog, a border collie that trotted ahead sniffing at the occasional lump of seaweed. The man stopped, and immediately the dog crouched, alert to the Frisbee in his outstretched arm. She watched for several minutes as the dog repeatedly retrieved the frisbee and delivered it to its master. This time the red disc spun through the air. The dog charged in the direction of the throw and launched itself for the catch. Suddenly, the Frisbee was caught by an onshore gust that propelled it backwards. In one fluid movement the dog pirouetted in midair and snatched the disc, landing perfectly on all four limbs. Trotting back to its master, the dog returned its prize nonchalantly. Isobel watched with admiration, allowing her frustration to be subdued by the dog's repeated success. Thus far on this trip she had achieved very little, but at least she had found her parents. Perhaps tomorrow she would find out something concrete about her *real* parents.

During Isobel's final year in college the topic of ancestry had come up during dinner one evening with her roommates. One of her roommates had taken an ancestry test and the results had just arrived. She was born in Ireland and had assumed that as her parents and grandparents were Irish, she must be too. The results had been a shock — she was only fifty percent Irish, the balance a mixture of Norwegian and Danish. The roommate had been skeptical of the results, and the discussion that evening had centered on whether these tests were accurate or useful. Opinions had differed, but everyone agreed they might be useful for discovering distant relatives.

The tests were expensive. Nonetheless, Isobel ordered one a few days later and sent off a sample of her DNA. She wasn't surprised with her results, especially as she already knew she had been born in Bosnia. She was definitely Slavic, with minor contributions from other parts of central Europe. Spurred by her initial investment and with the help of a professor of Slavic studies at the university, she began to search Slavic databases but quickly became frustrated. Many of the records AncestryDNA relied upon — birth, marriage, death, census — had been destroyed in the Bosnian War. In the end her search yielded nothing useful, and in the ensuing years no one had contacted her, claiming to be a relative.

The professor of Slavic studies had not meant to alarm her when he suggested that she might be a war baby. The term meant little to her at the time, but later she realized what he had insinuated, that her mother had been raped. The ugly idea had been seeded, and from then on it had lurked in the recesses of her mind, emerging when she felt most vulnerable.

~

It was quiet in the dining room that evening with just four other couples having dinner. Isobel chose a seat by the window overlooking the bay and ordered a glass of wine. The selection was extensive, with many of the labels from local vineyards. She hadn't realized that Nelson was a wine-growing region and found herself sampling a glass of Chardonnay. It was very different from the oaked California Chardonnays she was used to, but she liked its crisp flavor. The menu was a surprise too, with an emphasis on locally sourced meats and vegetables. Sipping her wine, she made a mental note to inquire at the reception desk as to where she could buy a bottle to bring with her to dinner at her parents' house the following evening. Back in her room, she wrote a long email to Vic describing the events of the day and asked him to come up with a time when they could talk. Up to now she had never doubted his commitment to her, but for some reason an unpleasant thought had wormed its way into her brain. If she called him now, would she find him at home, and if not, where was he?

The phone rang and she grabbed at it, expecting to hear Vic's voice. Instead, it was her mother.

"I just wanted to let you know not to come to dinner tomorrow. Your father is in the hospital, and they want to keep him for a few days."

"What's happened?" Isobel demanded, her heart plummeting in her chest.

"He started to have trouble breathing soon after you left. I turned up his oxygen, but it didn't make any difference. I decided the best thing was to drive him to the emergency room in Nelson. That's where we are now."

Isobel could hear the worry in her mother's voice. Briefly she considered driving to Nelson, but she had drunk two glasses of wine at dinner and knew it would be foolhardy.

"I'll come to the hospital first thing in the morning," she said, her tone urgent.

"Don't do that. You'll just complicate things."

Before she could stop herself, Isobel blurted out, "You've always tried to keep me away from him. Always. And now you're doing it again."

There was a gasp on the other end of the line. When her mother spoke again, her voice was strained.

"That is so unfair, Isobel. You have no idea...."

"How could I have any idea? You've never told me anything. I came all this way...and now..."

Her mother interrupted her, her voice now under control. "I *know* why you came here, Isobel."

Isobel held the phone tightly to her ear, listening to her mother's ragged breathing.

A minute passed, then her mother spoke again. "Right now, your father is in no fit state to have that conversation. He's got a mask clamped over his face and cannot talk to anyone. He can barely breathe." She gave a sigh. "This is the third time in two months we have gone through this...that *I've* gone through this."

Before her mother could continue, Isobel interrupted her. "What's wrong with Dad?"

She could hear her mother swallow before replying.

"He has cancer — a type of blood cancer. He's had it for a few years now. The chemo helped at first, but now there's nothing more they can do."

"Why didn't you tell me?" Isobel said. She had begun to cry.

"What good would it have done?"

The question hung in the air between them. A minute passed.

"Here's what I think is going to happen," her mother said in a tired voice. "They'll give him a blood transfusion, get him stabilized, then do dialysis. After that, if it's like the last time, they'll send him home. He'll have an oxygen mask most of that time, so it's useless trying to visit or talk. I'll call you if anything changes."

"What should *I* do?" Isobel asked. As soon as the words were out of her mouth, she realized how selfish she sounded.

"Oh, Isobel, I don't know," her mother said, sighing deeply. "Why don't you just go away for a few days.... Be a tourist or something."

Isobel sniffled audibly.

"Plan on coming to dinner next Thursday," her mother said in a more upbeat voice. "Your father should be home by then."

"And if he gets worse?"

"If he gets worse, I will call you."

Even though Isobel knew she should offer some words of comfort, she ended the conversation.

"Goodnight, Mom. I'll see you on Thursday."

CHAPTER 11

Five days. It seemed like an eternity. The previous week had passed in a rush, and now, suddenly, everything had come to a screeching halt. Nothing to do but wait.

Isobel had always prided herself on cramming more into a day than most. Being a university athlete just reinforced the traits she had developed as a child. Not content to complete a school assignment on time, she would get it finished early, then go to the local tennis court and hit balls for hours at a time. Her parents could find little reason to object for she was consistently an A student. At university she had always felt driven, be it a class assignment written in the back of the team bus on the way to a tennis tournament or cleaning out dog kennels at the veterinary clinic. Now, with nothing to do for five days, she was completely at a loss.

The same young woman who checked her in the previous day was at the reception desk when Isobel walked by after breakfast.

"Excuse me," Isobel said. "I was wondering...if you had

a few days to spend here in this part of New Zealand, what would you do? Where would *you* go?"

The emphasis was intended; Isobel thought she looked as if she would spend her free time outdoors.

The woman's face lit up as if she had been given a gift of a few days' vacation herself.

"I'd go up to Abel Tasman, of course. Believe me, there's no place like it in the world. And a few days is way too short, but it'll give you a taste."

Isobel nodded. "Okay. I guess I don't know anything about the place. I know it's a National Park, but that's about it." She gave the receptionist a questioning look. "What about biking? I saw some bike paths on the way here."

"Yes. There's biking. But I'd still go to Abel Tasman."

She came out from behind her desk and walked to a stand in the foyer. Selecting a brochure from several arrayed on the stand, she handed it to Isobel.

"This'll give you an idea of what the park is like."

"Em. Any particular recommendations?" Isobel asked.

The woman scanned the foyer, then leaned towards Isobel, her voice barely a whisper.

"I know we're not meant to push one tour operator more than another, but if I were you, I'd drive into town and go to Stan's Place. It's on the main street — you'll see the sign."

Noticing the doubtful expression on Isobel's face, she added, "Yep, it's called Stan's Place." She gave a little laugh. "Stan Townsend is the best tour operator around. They'll set you right, whether you have a day or a month."

Back in her room, Isobel looked through the brochure, a simple colorful trifold. The banner title read, Abel Tasman National Park and Golden Bay. Beneath the miniature map, which showed the park's location on the northern tip of

South Island, there was a brief description. "Breathtaking scenery is no cliché" caught her eye. Opening her computer, she brought up a much larger map of the region. Bordered by the coastline, the park was small by comparison with other parks on South Island and strikingly devoid of access roads to the interior. Instead, numerous boat landing sites dotted the coastline. Zooming in, she searched for her hotel as a point of reference, then moved the image on the screen to the left until she came to the main street of Kaiteriteri. Stan's Place was clearly marked, next to a knife and fork symbol for the Beached Whale Restaurant and Bar. Picking up her keys and purse, she walked briskly to the parking lot.

Even though it was after eleven, the town seemed deserted. Stan's Place was easy to find, and Isobel pulled into the empty lot on the side of the building. Walking around to the front, she was reassured to see a rack of clothing on the sidewalk with "Sale" displayed prominently above it. In her experience, shops in resort towns out of season kept irregular hours, and season might not mean the same thing in New Zealand as it did in North America. She hadn't spent any time researching the weather in the southern hemisphere before leaving Wisconsin. Jeans, sweatpants, T-shirts, a fleece, and a raincoat covered all eventualities, and if necessary she could buy whatever else she needed. As if to reassure her, the familiar logos of Patagonia, Columbia, Rav, and North Face were plastered on the bottom of the two large windows that faced the street. Peering in, she noted equipment for every outdoor sport — mountain bikes, paddleboards, rock climbing equipment, and scuba gear. A dog lay sleeping on the pavement just outside the door, barely opening its eyes as she stepped over it and went inside.

"*Kia Ora.* Can I help you?" came a muffled voice from somewhere in the back of the cluttered room.

Isobel raised her voice, hoping it would carry.

"Hi. I'm looking for Stan. The woman at the reception desk at the Eco Lodge told me to ask for him. She said he's the best person to ask about going to Abel Tasman."

She waited patiently for the person to appear, expecting to see a man, likely between the ages of thirty and forty, with a weather-beaten face and a lean muscular body. He might have longish hair or a ponytail, and he would be wearing comfortable outdoorsy clothes. On his feet would be hiking boots or sandals. She smiled inwardly realizing she had just conjured an image of Vic. The person who appeared was none of those things. Nowhere in her imagination could Isobel have come up with the individual who emerged from the back of the store and greeted her.

"I'm Stan. And she's right about Abel Tasman. What can I do for you, luvvy?"

Isobel tried to guess the woman's age but failed. She was short and rotund and wore a long flowing dress that hid whatever deformity caused a pronounced limp. Her short, spiky hair was mostly green with a patch of pink near the right temple. Pudgy arms ended in wrists that were festooned with bangles, and on most of her fingers and both thumbs she wore demonstrative silvery rings. The sandals peeking out from beneath the hem of her dress gave Isobel a tiny feeling of satisfaction. At least she got one thing right.

Isobel couldn't help fixating on the woman's face. She had a *Tā moko* — the traditional Maori facial tattoo. Extending from the tip of her chin to her lower lip, a symmetrical pattern of black curled shapes swept upwards, each of them ending in a sharp point. They look like a collection of miniature scimitars. The woman's full-shaped lips were almost black, contrasting with her brown complexion and dark heavy eyebrows that emphasized the green and pink of her hair.

Much as she tried, Isobel could not hide the look of incredulity that had come over her face. Stan burst out laughing, a sound that erupted from deep within her chest and caused her pendulous breasts to move alarmingly.

"I know. Nobody expects Stan to be a woman, but there you are. As for the dress, well, it's low season so who's to mind? It's a dull sorta day and I needed to cheer meself up. It's very comfortable, by the way. As for the hair, I tried the green dye last week, but it made me look like a grinch. The pink is better, don't you think? But it's a bit Barbie. No worries. It'll fade soon enough. Then I'll be...mmm...hope it's not gone gray yet."

She looked down at her hands, spreading the fingers wide.

"As for this lot, I don't wear jewelry when I'm out working. I like buying it, though. I see a piece and think, Gawd, that's lovely. I *want* that — a bit like Gollum. So I get it, and it ends up in a drawer somewhere, never seeing the light of day." She gave a sniff. "Well, today is the 'light of day' and every piece of jewelry I own is getting a chance to bask in it. Now, where were we? Oh yes, what did Di at the Lodge think you might be interested in?"

Isobel couldn't help smiling. If nothing else, she would have fun telling Vic about this encounter whenever she finally got a chance to talk to him.

"Hi. I'm Isobel." She held out her hand, which, to the accompaniment of jingling, was grasped firmly; she could feel each of the rings.

"I have a few days to spare before...a meeting next Thursday, and I'd like to see something of the area. The woman at the reception desk gave me a brochure about the park, but then said I should talk with you — that you'd have some ideas."

Stan cocked her head to one side. "Well, it's not the best time of year for sitting on a beach sunbathing, is it? So, what are you into? Hiking or fishing or...what?"

Her forehead creased, the dark eyebrows almost touching, and Isobel couldn't help noticing how the tattoo changed shape as she spoke.

"Hiking. I like hiking."

"How about camping?"

"Camping's fine too."

"How many days did you say you have?"

Isobel thought for a moment before replying. "I have to be in Motueka on Thursday afternoon."

Stan gave a sigh. She moved her head from side to side as if she were stretching her neck muscles, then stretched her hands above her head, twisting the interlocked fingers and making the bracelets jingle. Isobel waited impatiently, trying not to focus on the *moko*.

"How about this? I can take you on a three-night/four-day adventure: hiking, camping, maybe even a bit of fishing. We'll get dropped off by boat and picked up by car, so we can go more or less anywhere. It won't be expensive — definitely a lot cheaper than staying up at that fancy hotel for three nights. I look after the food, and I'm a pretty good camp cook." She pointed a finger at Isobel. "You can carry the wine."

The raucous laugh erupted again. "Only joking. I carry most everything for my guests."

Isobel's eyes widened. An hour ago she had felt frustrated, wondering how she might occupy herself until Thursday. Suddenly, she was being asked if she wanted to spend four days in a wilderness with this strange individual.

"Come on, luvvy, make up your mind. I can see you're the sort of person who has to agonize their way through everything, line up all the options and consequences. For fuck's sake, it's only a hike. You'll be in much better shape for that meeting by the time we get back, mentally and physically."

"How about something shorter, like a day hike, or maybe one overnight?" Isobel gave a half smile.

The look on Stan's face made it clear that this was not the correct answer. Looking away from Isobel, she tapped her foot, her body language shouting impatience.

"Sure. Why not; let's go for the four days," Isobel said finally, trying to infuse some enthusiasm into her voice.

"Good on ya! Now, let's get down to business."

Chapter 12

Isobel returned to the hotel and spent some time reading about the Abel Tasman Coast Track. The brochures she had downloaded showed white sands, turquoise waters, sunny skies, and the smiling faces of hikers and kayakers. Most people who ventured to the park spent five or more days hiking the forty-mile trail, whereas Stan had proposed they hike just the middle section. Later that afternoon Isobel walked into town to get a sense of the air temperature. It felt much like a fall day in Wisconsin — cool and damp, but not unpleasant. Her reward was a basket of fish and chips and glass of wine at the Beached Whale where the barman already knew of her plans.

"So, you're off with Stan tomorrow," he said, placing her drink on the counter. "You'll have a wild and wooly time, I reckon." He winked.

Sipping her wine, Isobel went over her last conversation with Stan about their plans for the following day.

Stan had looked Isobel up and down and muttered something to the effect, "You're not one of those hoity-toity ones, are you? 'Cos if so, I'm not so sure this is going to work."

Isobel had assured her she was in good physical shape, had previously been on a university tennis team, and had kept up a regime of regular exercise since college.

"I brought hiking boots with me," Isobel had informed Stan, a note of pride in her voice.

"Well, good for you. Did you tuck them in beside the Manolo Blahniks?"

Isobel's eyes flashed at the mention of expensive high heels, and a corner of Stan's mouth lifted in response, the *moko* scimitars almost clashing.

"C'mon luvvy. I was only joking." She shrugged. "It's just my way. Don't give it a thought."

A backpack and suitable clothing for a multiday hike in a coastal area in spring presented a different problem. Isobel hadn't brought clothes for that, nor did she especially want to purchase a full wardrobe of designer labels at Stan's Place. With another eye-catching facial expression, Stan had pointed out that she and Isobel were not the same size. Fortunately, she had previous clients who were less pecuniary, as well as reluctant to haul their slightly used but muddied gear back to their home countries. As a result, there was a storage locker at the back of the shop full of castoffs, which Stan happily re-issued at a marginal cost.

"I give the rental money to the Coastguard Association. God knows but they've earned it, hauled me out of a few tricky situations over the years."

The forecast was for temperatures hovering in the mid-fifties during the day and dropping ten to twenty degrees at night. Rain was a possibility.

"You can leave your luggage at the hotel," Stan advised her. "Di's used to folks doing that and doesn't charge. She trusts I'll bring you back safe and sound and knows damn well you'll want to stay there when it's over. Creature comforts and all that. Hah." She gave a snort, adding, "My record is still a hundred percent, though not always in the specified time. There was a client once.... Nah. You don't need to hear that story."

~

The following day Isobel found herself carrying a well-fitting pack that weighed around twenty-five pounds. As she looked at Stan's huge pack, she estimated it must weigh sixty pounds and marveled that the woman could lift it from the floor, let alone hoist it on her squat frame. Somehow it seemed to even out her limp, and Isobel wondered if she had packed it in such a way as to achieve just that outcome.

"Are you sure you don't want me to take more in my pack?" Isobel asked.

"Nah, luvvy. Can't have the clients complaining on their first day. Maybe tomorrow we can switch, eh?" She gave a laugh. Her breasts were trapped within the cross strap of the pack and this time they obediently stayed in place.

With reassuring efficiency, Stan had chosen their start point, the route they would hike, and where and when they would be picked up. She had organized their meals, the clothes Isobel would need, their sleeping bags, and two small tents.

"I never share with a guest." Stan smirked knowingly. "It's not professional. Then again, sometimes I like to share." Scrutinizing Isobel from head to toe, she added, "Don't worry, luvvy. You're not my type."

Isobel had wanted to reply, "You're not mine either," but thought better of it. She was going to be relying on this person for everything for the next few days and wanted to make sure things went smoothly.

They walked to a boat ramp where a black inflatable was moored, a sign on the side announcing Abel Tasman Aqua Taxi. A middle-aged man climbed up onto the jetty to greet them.

"*Kia Ora*, Stan. I see you found another excuse for not working in the shop. You take more vacations than anyone else I know around here. It's a miracle you stay in business."

"Speak for yourself, Jeff. Aren't you just back from the sun, sea, and sand of Thailand? Hope that was all you got there…or brought back, for that matter."

The bantering continued as they loaded the inflatable, but despite Stan's ever-increasing accusations of Jeff indulging in many of the seven deadly sins in Thailand, it was clear to Isobel they held a deep-seated mutual respect as well as considerable affection.

They cast off and motored out into a slightly choppy sea. Reassuringly large patches of blue sky were interspersed with a few clouds, the shape of which meant nothing to Isobel. She had grown up in a city where shelter was readily available if it rained or snowed. Wisconsin was different, but as most of the weather came from states lying to the west, there was always ample time to prepare for storms. As they passed a small island at the mouth of the bay, Isobel looked back towards Kaiteriteri. She could just make out the hotel where she had enjoyed luxurious accommodation and fine dining. The coming days and nights were going to be very different.

It had been a long time since Isobel had allowed someone else to make all the decisions for her. It wasn't something she was accustomed to, not since that summer after her first year in college when she had had to swallow the bitter pill of knowing she alone was responsible for her life. Responsibility was a burden she accepted, if reluctantly. The only person she had ever felt she could securely relinquish it to was Vic, the reason being that he didn't see responsibility as a burden at all. Instead, he took it upon himself effortlessly, as if caring for others was his purpose in life. He had been that way with Maggie. Isobel thought back to the first time she met him. It had been Maggie's idea, of course. When Isobel was clearing out the guesthouse, Maggie suggested that Vic could help her disassembling the heavy metal bookshelves in the basement. He came over a few days later, and they spent several hours working on the project. She had enjoyed it, mostly because he followed her directions and didn't argue or suggest a better way of doing things, as most men were inclined to do. He was quiet, competent, and surprisingly respectful. Afterwards, Maggie insisted they both have dinner with her that evening. She pointed out to Vic that Isobel was now doing all of her cooking, and he complimented her on the excellent meal. Old-fashioned was the word she used later that evening to describe him to one of her roommates in Madison. Old-fashioned and nice, and good-looking too.

Throughout that summer Vic came by Maggie's house regularly to mow the fire breaks around the prairie. Little by little Isobel's relationship with him developed and deepened. Initially their conversations had revolved around Maggie, but gradually they strayed into talking about themselves. She already knew quite a lot about Vic — his youthful waywardness and how, with the help of Maggie and her husband, he had turned things around and now owned his own construction business.

She thought back to the first night they spent together. It was the day she moved into Maggie's guesthouse, renting the place for a semester while she took prerequisite classes for veterinary school. Vic had helped her move her things from

Madison. Everything she owned fitted easily into the back of his pickup truck.

When they had finished, she opened a bottle of wine and poured a glass for each of them.

"Here's to my new life...to getting into veterinary school... and to Maggie, without whom none of this would have happened."

Vic was sitting in the wing-backed chair by the window that overlooked the prairie; she was sitting on the couch, Oliver at her feet. With easy confidence he got up from his chair and joined her. Taking her glass from her hand, he placed it on the coffee table and turned to her.

"I think it's about time, don't you?" he said and kissed her.

The remainder of the evening felt as natural and easy as if they had always been together.

Isobel sighed. She had tried to call Vic again last night, counting the unanswered rings and finally giving up, not bothering to leave a message. Where was he? She wasn't a jealous person by nature, but the absence of reassurance that he still loved her, combined with the thousands of miles that separated them, resurrected the feelings of abandonment she had spent years learning to suppress.

His last email had been businesslike. She knew he was always overcommitted and rarely had time to write a long message, but still, she would have liked something more intimate. Her reply had been equally brief, letting him know she would be away for the next three days, hiking in Abel Tasman National Park with a guide. She had finished with "I'll catch up with you when I get back" and debated with herself how best to sign off. Suppressing the voice in her head that wanted to shout,

"Where the hell are you?" she opted for a more neutral, "Love you," and pressed send.

∼

An hour later Jeff cut back on the throttle and maneuvered the inflatable into the jetty at Torrent Bay.

"I'll see you on Wednesday at Whainui, yes?" he asked as he handed Stan's pack up to her.

"That's right. Four days from now. It'll give you time to work on that tan of yours."

He grinned back at her. "Yeah, yeah. Ladies love it."

He turned to Isobel, who was standing on the jetty beside her pack.

"Don't worry. You'll have a great time. Stan's the best."

Stan's laugh erupted. "You were always a liar, Jeff, just not a good one."

He backed the inflatable away from the jetty, turned it around, and headed out to sea. With a roar of the engine, the nose of the boat lifted out of the water, its wake like an arrow pointing south.

Chapter 13

As the day progressed, most of Isobel's worries dissipated. Here she was in one of the most beautiful places on earth, young, strong, capable, and with enough money to not have to worry about wasting these days before she could see her parents again. What an amazing gift Maggie had given her. She slowed down to leave a generous gap between herself and Stan. She wanted to talk to Maggie, out loud.

"Well, Maggie, what do you think?"

Isobel listened to the silence, hunting for the soft Irish cadence of the elderly woman's voice.

The scenery is lovely. A bit like the west of Ireland, up around County Sligo that has those wide-open beaches and nobody on them. The weather's a bit like Ireland too. You'll not be getting a tan on this walk.

"I'm feeling a bit lost right now. I'm not sure I did the right thing coming here. Maybe I should have waited like Vic said and started vet school. Do you think I've messed up my career?"

Oh, for Heaven's sake, Isobel, don't be so dramatic. You've always wanted to find out why your mother gave you up for adoption, why she "abandoned" you as you like to say. Well, in the next few days you'll either find out or you won't. One way or the other, you'll be able to turn your attention to getting on with your life, which is actually the most important thing.

"Yeah. But what happens if I don't get into vet school next year?"

Isobel could almost hear the sigh of exasperation.

Remember last year when we talked about the importance of always having a backup plan? You had one then, didn't you? You were going to do a master's in public health if you didn't get a place in vet school. You got accepted to that program too but declined. Well, make sure you apply to the MPH program as well as vet school this time. One of them is bound to come through.

Look, these are just forks in the road. A bit like the signposts on this track. You go left, you end up in one place; you go right, you end up somewhere else. Neither is right or wrong, better or worse — it's what you choose to make of it. Besides, you'll never know what life would have been like had you taken that other track, turned left instead of right. Be happy with the one you're on.

A shout from Stan interrupted Isobel's conversation.

"Hey, you! Am I going to have to listen to you mumbling away to yourself for the next three days?"

Isobel caught up with Stan, who had stopped, hands on hips and one foot tapping the ground. So intent had she been in her conversation with Maggie that she hadn't noticed the spectacular scenery surrounding them. They had hiked uphill, past a jungle of ferns, low shrubs, and moss-covered boulders and were now looking down on a bay where a turquoise pool of water beckoned.

"It's cold enough to freeze the balls off a brass monkey, but I'm going in," Stan said, making a rude gesture to indicate what she meant.

Isobel followed her down the steep path to the water and watched as she flung off her pack and within moments had divested herself of all her clothes. She thrashed her way into the water singing, "Bye, bye Miss American Pie," at the top of her lungs. "This'll be the day that I die...this'll be the day that I die."

Isobel took off her pack, relieved to be rid of the unaccustomed weight that left her breasts feeling sore. Before she could make a decision whether to join Stan, the woman re-emerged from the water like a strange sea creature with a pink and green crest, ran up the beach to where she had left her pack, and pulled out a colorful towel, which she managed to wrap all the way around her generous body.

"That was bloody brilliant," she said through gray lips. Then, with exquisite efficiency, she pulled her clothes on and spread the towel over a nearby bush. Diving into her pack again, she rummaged around and pulled out a tiny stove, a pot, and a plastic container.

"Soup. Just the thing to warm our...cockles." She gave one of her characteristic deep, rumbling laughs and began to prepare their lunch.

"I made it last night — chicken noodle. It always works. Well, except for vegetarians. Another bunch of wankers. I mean, I don't mind *why* they're doing it — methane and climate warming and all that; it's just such a nuisance to always be thinking, can they eat this? or are they allergic and going to die on the trail on me? As for vegans...I just don't take them." She shook her head vehemently.

The soup settled comfortably in Isobel's stomach, giving

her a sense of well-being. Sitting on a rock close to the water's edge, she took the time to look around. In front of her the water was a crystal-clear shade of blue merging into a pale yellow where it met the pristine sand. Behind her a veneer of vibrant green foliage clung to the rocky promontory they had hiked down. She felt as if she were a castaway...a castaway with a personal assistant. That image prompted a spontaneous chuckle.

"Yeah?" Stan looked over at her inquiringly. "What's so funny?"

"I was just thinking how perfect this spot is. Makes me forget what I'm doing here."

"What *are* you doing here?"

Isobel considered for a moment before answering. The directness of Stan's question had taken her aback.

"Passing time, I suppose...until I get to the next thing." She forced a smile.

"Seems like a terrible waste to me. I mean, *now* is where we are. The present. This moment. Why would you let it pass? I tell you, I'm sucking everything I can out of it. Sucking it dry, and it tastes great!"

Isobel felt resentment, then anger. Stan's outburst had struck home, like a poorly aimed arrow that had somehow hit the bull's-eye. She snapped back, "Who are you to tell me how to live my life?"

Stan eyes widened, and she glared at Isobel, her dark eyebrows raised threateningly.

"I'm not telling you how to live *your* life. I'm telling you how I live *mine*."

Her eyebrows relaxed. She held out her hands, palms upward.

"Okay. I apologize. You're the guest, and I'm the guide."

With her back turned to Isobel, she packed the stove and the pot, then hoisted her pack.

"We should get going," she said, her voice lacking emotion.

~

The bottle of wine they shared that evening helped to soften the prickly atmosphere. The two women sat in silence, staring into the embers of the fire while the rhythmic drum of waves pulsed in the background. Something about the remoteness of the place, the unfamiliarity of the southern sky with its myriad stars, and a sense of exhausted well-being coupled with wine compelled Isobel to clarify her earlier statement. She was embarrassed by what she had said, "Passing time until I get to the next thing." Those asinine words had bounced around her brain for the remainder of the afternoon, and she realized she must have sounded like a spoiled rich kid — the type of guest Stan despised.

At pains to dispel that image, she gave Stan a rough outline of how she had come to be in this part of New Zealand and why it was she had a few days with nothing to do but wait. She chose her words carefully, listening to how she was portraying her situation. She couldn't see Stan's face, but nonetheless, it was a relief to have someone real to talk to as opposed to a ghost. Isobel found herself admitting how hard it was to stop thinking about the next meeting with her father and how their conversation might go. Would he finally tell her what she had come all this way for? Whether Stan was listening or not became less important than Isobel hearing her own story presented aloud. In the darkness, what she had done didn't sound so irresponsible.

For the past few weeks, some internal knell had forced Isobel awake each night, and she would lie in bed for two or three hours yearning for a reprieve. This night was different; she slept more soundly than any night since Maggie's death. She woke once and thought about going to the bathroom but decided it wasn't urgent enough to crawl out of a warm sleeping bag. Instead, she nestled farther down into its tight embrace, her mind at peace.

Chapter 14

Mindful of the conversation she and Stan had the previous evening, instead of dwelling on the upcoming meeting with her parents, Isobel concentrated on trying to appreciate each step of the hike — smells, sounds, the profusion of greenery, the narrow line of trail wending its way into the unknown. Hours and minutes stretched and contracted without reference to any external markers, while overcast skies deprived her of even the most rudimentary chronometric signals. Like most of her generation, Isobel was accustomed to checking her cell phone regularly. But with Stan's reminder that there would be no signal on the trail, she had deliberately stowed it in her pack.

"I saw you looking at your phone before we left this morning," Stan remarked. "So, who's at home waiting for you?"

They were sitting side by side on a massive tree trunk bleached by the ocean over many seasons. Even though she had become accustomed to Stan's peremptory style, Isobel was taken aback by the question. She hadn't been thinking about Vic, but prompted by Stan's question, images of her boyfriend paraded through her mind like hearts and cherries and numbers in a slot machine. When the spinning stopped, she saw three images of Vic's face in a row. They were identical. It was how he looked the day she told him she was going to New Zealand, his expression one of disapproval. What was it he had said that day? That it was a dumb idea. He hadn't given her any encouragement, not then or in the weeks before she left.

"Well, I live with a guy called Vic. We've been together for over a year now." Isobel's voice softened. "He's a really good guy." She paused to look at a gull that was pecking at a piece of driftwood.

"Yeah?" Stan prompted. "He's 'the one' then?"

Isobel found herself unwilling to answer Stan's question. She was no longer sure.

"It all began when I started working for this elderly lady called Maggie, who needed help because she had fallen down the stairs in her house and broken some bones. Vic used to hang around her place when he was a kid. When he grew up — her husband had died by then — he'd check in on her, make sure she was doing okay. Fix things, mow the grass, and plow snow in winter. That sort of stuff. He even reroofed her barn. He was very fond of her." She gave a little sniff. "She died a month ago."

Stan said nothing. Isobel resumed her story, describing how she had met and ultimately fallen in love with Vic.

"So why didn't he come to New Zealand with you? By the sounds of things, he'd have liked it here." She made a sweeping gesture with her hand to indicate the bay with the ocean beyond.

"He's working. He does construction, so he can't just leave, even though he's the boss. Besides, he understands why I need to do this alone."

Even as she said this, Isobel realized it wasn't true. Vic

didn't understand. It was something she herself found difficult to explain — this gut-wrenching desire to know who her parents were and why they had given their daughter away.

Standing up, Isobel gave a long sigh. "I'll call him when we get to the pickup place. You said there was a signal there, didn't you? The time difference between here and Wisconsin makes it really awkward, and every time I've called so far, there's been no answer."

"Silence is underrated," said Stan. Isobel wasn't sure if the comment was meant for her. She decided to ignore it.

∼

Lying in her sleeping bag that night, Isobel found herself thinking more critically about Vic. It was something Stan had said...about him being "the one." She had never questioned that he was the right person for her until now. Their relationship had seemed so natural and easy, especially under Maggie's fond gaze. But if Maggie had not been in the picture, would she have felt the same way about Vic? She had surprised herself by flirting with Paul at Luke's Kitchen and going back to the restaurant the following morning to see if he was there. What did this say about her relationship with Vic? Was he the person she wanted to spend the rest of her life with?

Sleep continued to elude her, and for a while she allowed herself to toy with the idea of a different life. What if she never went back to Wisconsin? It wasn't an impossible notion. As the daughter of someone born in New Zealand, she could apply for citizenship, and with her university qualifications and experience, she was sure she would find a job. Perhaps she could even apply to veterinary school here. Isobel pushed these thoughts out of her mind and tried to resurrect a more positive image of Vic.

∼

On the final evening of their hike the temperature dropped, but sitting on a log beside the campfire with a mug of tea in her hand, Isobel felt warm and relaxed. Up to now she had hesitated to ask Stan about herself, but after their days together she felt emboldened.

"How did you get into guiding, Stan? Are you from South Island?"

"Nah. I was born in Northland, near Whangarei. That's north of Auckland. My *iwi* — my tribe — is *Ngāpuhi*. I went to school, had a couple of years at uni, but didn't like it much. Went traveling around southeast Asia for a few years, met a guy, and we came back to New Zealand."

Isobel noticed Stan was fidgeting with imaginary rings.

"We lived in Wellington for a few years, then he up and left. It was just as well."

Stan stopped talking abruptly. Isobel waited for her to continue, then said jokingly, "So he wasn't 'the one,' then?"

She could see Stan's shoulders tense and immediately regretted asking the question.

"He was a brute."

This time the silence lasted several minutes. Then Stan shook her head vigorously as if to rid herself of vermin. Taking a sip of tea, she continued.

"I was working at the National Museum then. I liked the job well enough, but Wellington's a big city and not where I wanted to end up. So, I came down here to Kaiteriteri and started Stan's Place. The rest is history, I suppose."

"How long have you been down here?"

"Almost seventeen years. I was twenty-eight when I left Wellington."

Isobel tried to imagine the man Stan called a brute. Was he a Maori, she wondered? Had he hit her? Was he the reason Stan had a limp? Was that why she had a *moko*?

"Can I ask you about your *moko*?"

The moment the words left her mouth Isobel regretted them. She backpedaled quickly.

"I read about *moko* in the Air New Zealand magazine on the plane. The article suggested that these days it's not just about ancestors but also empowerment...of Maori women especially."

Isobel hoped she had moderated her impertinence. Nonetheless, there was another question she wanted to ask. She tried to be diplomatic.

"I read that it's a coming-of-age thing — a passage between being a girl and an adult. I was curious about one thing, though. What age were you when you got it?"

"You're right about the coming-of-age thing, only it took me a lot longer to do that — mature, I mean. I got mine at twenty-seven."

Remembering what Stan had said earlier, Isobel calculated it would have been around the time the man she had called a brute left.

"I've just turned twenty-seven."

"Yeah, well, you're way ahead of where I was at your age."

Another silence, during which Isobel's thoughts turned to Vic. The slot machine spun again, this time presenting her with three reassuring images of Vic's smiling face.

"Did it hurt a lot?" Isobel winced slightly, glad that it was too dark for Stan to notice.

"Nah. I was psyched. I lay there for six hours, a hunk of orange in my mouth to bite on. Afterwards I felt different. Now, every time I look at myself in a mirror, I'm reminded that my *tupuna*, my ancestors, have my back."

Isobel would have liked to know more about Stan's life. More than anything, she wanted to know how this fascinating woman had acquired such strength and resilience — qualities that Isobel yearned to have. But the woman's body language made clear their conversation was over. Her guide stood up, stretched her arms above her head, and twisted her body from side to side. Isobel watched as she spread the last of the embers, doused them with a can of sea water, and limped towards her tent.

Chapter 15

Just before noon the following day, they arrived at the parking lot where they would rendezvous with Jeff. The previous hours of hiking had been idyllic, from when they broke camp and started walking at first light, to rounding the final headland and breathing in the immensity of the ocean. Early morning was a magical time, one that Isobel rarely had the opportunity to savor in Wisconsin; there was always a list and never enough time to stop and breathe, to appreciate the quality of those first rays of light, the distinctive aroma of soil as it warmed. The past few days had allowed her to do just that. But the hike had also forced her to explore an alternative narrative, leaving her confused about her relationship with Vic.

With the end of the hike approaching, she turned her thoughts to the upcoming dinner with her parents and imagined how the evening might go, assuming her father was out of hospital and able to talk. He would finally tell her everything, and she could go home. Or he would continue to refuse, and she would go home having wasted not just a lot of Maggie's money but perhaps also her chance to go to vet school. There was another, worst-case scenario: her father dying in the hospital. In that event, would her mother be willing to tell her?

Stan was walking purposefully towards a green Toyota Land Cruiser, already undoing the waist strap of her pack. By the time Isobel caught up with her, Jeff had loaded the pack into the back of the vehicle, and she and Jeff were already bantering.

"C'mon. Let's get going. I've not got all day to entertain you two ladies."

They climbed into the Land Cruiser and drove out of the parking lot through a Maori-styled ceremonial gate. It would take another hour on winding roads to drive back to Kaiteriteri, but Stan insisted they stop for lunch along the way.

"I'd murder for a flat white and a pizza right now," she said. "How about you?"

The question was directed towards Isobel, who agreed readily. Despite Stan's culinary expertise over the previous few days, the thought of a burger and fries made Isobel's stomach rumble. They ate lunch at a small café called "The Last Gasp" where Isobel satisfied her craving for salt and fat after days of abstinence.

"Aren't you going to call the keeper then, luvvy? It's coming up on three p.m."

Isobel looked at Stan, a puzzled expression on her face. "The keeper?"

"Don't tell me you've forgotten him already. You know, 'The keeper. The one.'" She made a rude gesture with her fingers. "The guy who's keeping your bed warm. What's his name? You told me yesterday, but I've already forgotten."

"Vic."

"That's it. Vic. You've got time to call him before we head

back. There's good cell service here. Go ahead. We won't listen, will we Jeff?"

She gave an exaggerated shake of her head from side to side, mouthing the word "No."

"Wouldn't think of it," he replied, cupping his hands behind his ears.

Isobel moved to a bench near the water's edge, just down from the restaurant patio. She dialed the familiar number and waited. Whether it was the anticipation or the rapidly consumed lunch, she felt a little nauseous.

"Isobel!" It was Vic. "Is that you? Where are you? I've missed you so much."

The words came out in a rush, leaving no opportunity for her to say anything. She waited, not sure if he had finished.

"Isobel, are you there...?"

"Yes, I'm here."

"Oh, it's *so* good to hear your voice. So, what's been happening? Did you find out anything more?"

"Slow down, slow down," she said, a wave of relief flooding through her at the sound of his voice. Maybe all of her misgivings had been a mistake. "I'm not sure where I left off or what was in my last email. I told you about finding Mom and Dad in a place called Motueka. It's on South Island, near Nelson. They invited me for dinner the next evening..." She let out a low whistle. "God, that was only five days ago; it feels like a lifetime. At any rate, Mum had to take Dad to the hospital that night. She called me and said not to come, that he'd be in hospital for a few days. He's on oxygen, wearing a mask so he can't talk. I'm going back tomorrow for dinner."

"Were they surprised to see you?"

"Yeah. Mum opened the door and just stood there when she saw me, like I was a ghost."

"Well, at least you found them, and hopefully your dad will be well enough to talk with you tomorrow." He paused. "So, you might be coming home soon?"

Isobel could hear the plaintive note in his voice.

"I don't know. I presume he'll be out of hospital, but what if he isn't? What if he can't talk to me?"

Vic's voice was soothing. "I'm sure it'll work out."

Neither of them said anything, each waiting for the other to speak.

"This place is empty without you. Oliver mopes when I let him out in the morning."

She laughed, imagining the look on Oliver's face as Vic opened the door each morning, too rushed to accompany the dog on the customary walk around the prairie.

"Where are you now?" Vic asked. Isobel tried to remember if she had told him about the hike.

"I thought I told you. I've just spent four days hiking on the Abel Tasman Coastal Trail. There was no point in hanging around the hotel, so I hired a guide and went tramping. That's what they call it here, tramping."

Isobel wasn't sure how to broach the next topic.

"I tried calling you a few times last week before I went on the hike, but there was no reply. I know with the time difference it's really awkward, but I didn't think you'd be out late three nights in a row." There was an accusatory ring to her comment.

"I've been spending evenings up at Maggie's, doing some work on the cabin. It really needs it."

"Well, that explains it," she said with relief. "The next time I call, I'll try Maggie's if I don't get you at our place."

"Nah. That won't work. I had the phone disconnected at Maggie's."

"Why did you do that?"

"Well, there's nobody living there now, and it costs a lot — over a hundred dollars each month. Don't you remember, she had a DSL line put in when you started to work for her?"

"That's not so much," Isobel said, "especially if you're spending a lot of time there. How am I meant to get a hold of you?"

"A hundred dollars a month might not be a lot to you these days, but it is for me."

Isobel noted the sudden change in Vic's tone. "Is there anything wrong? You sound upset about something."

"Well, of course I'm upset. You're not here."

She searched for something neutral to say. "Is Oliver behaving himself?"

The smile returned to Vic's voice. "Yeah. He's a good buddy. He comes to Maggie's with me all the time. At first he couldn't settle down. He'd go into each room looking for her, but I think he's finally realized she's not coming back."

There was another pause, then a sharp intake of breath, as if he were gearing up to deliver some unpleasant news.

"I got a letter from a lawyer in Massachusetts last week. He said he's representing Grace Mangan. Remember? That's Lara's real name, or at least the name she goes by nowadays. It's a good thing Maggie isn't here to witness what her daughter is up to. Lara claims I got the property illegally, that I pressured Maggie into giving it to me."

"What! That's ridiculous. Maggie signed the place over to you fair and square. Lara, or Grace, or whatever her name is, has no claim on it. Sure, she's Maggie's daughter, but she's never been in Maggie's life, never had any contact with her until I brought them together. And that didn't go well. She just resents the fact that *you* became Maggie's de facto son...and she...well, she was given up for adoption."

"I know all that, but I still have to respond, get another lawyer involved, and that costs money."

"Can't you just ignore it?"

"I'm afraid to. What if I do nothing and end up losing this place? Just because her claim is a lie doesn't mean it'll go away. Lies have a lot of power these days."

Isobel could hear fear in his voice. For a brief moment she regretted ever having introduced Lara into Maggie's life. It had brought joy initially, but now....

"I can loan you money for the lawyer."

She waited for Vic's response, knowing the conversation was heading in an uncomfortable direction. Like many midwestern men who had been imbued with strong Lutheran sensibilities, the thought of asking someone for financial help was anathema to him.

"I can't take money from you. It wouldn't be right."

Funny how lies catch up with you, Isobel thought. Had she been honest with Vic and told him that Maggie had given her fifty thousand dollars to go to New Zealand, not twenty-five thousand, it would be easy to persuade him to accept a loan. Now she would have to pretend she was dipping into her vet school money. On paper it might seem the same, but the emotional baggage was very different. She struggled to come up with a persuasive argument.

"For heaven's sake, Vic, Maggie was nothing if not practical when it came to money. Remember when she and I were selling all of her husband's stuff in the guesthouse? She drove a hard bargain. And as for her dealing with Bill Breunig, she didn't hesitate to hire a lawyer to sort that out. No. You are going to go back to Maggie's lawyer and get him to deal with the letter from Massachusetts." She tried to moderate the exasperation in her voice.

"Damn, I wish you were here, Isobel." He sighed heavily. "But I hear you. I'll call Richard tomorrow and arrange a meeting. See what the next step is. I don't know what to say except...thank you. You know I'll pay you back."

"Yes. I do. So stop worrying. It will all work out in the end."

"I love you."

"Yeah. Me too. Look, I've got to go. My ride is waiting."

She hung up before Vic could say anything else. She already had enough to worry about without Vic's problems. As soon as she got back to Kaiteriteri, she would need to call her mother and make sure that dinner with her parents was still on.

Chapter 16

Instead of parking on the road, Isobel pulled into the driveway of her parents' house. Her heart was pounding as she reached for the doorbell, but before she could raise her arm, the door swung open. Despite the welcoming smile, Isobel could see the stress etched into her mother's face.

"We saw the car drive up. Come in, come in. Your father is looking forward to seeing you. He's in the sitting room waiting for you. I'll join you in a minute. I just need to check on dinner."

To her surprise her father was not in his wheelchair. Instead, he sat in a large armchair, a throw covering his shrunken legs. The wheelchair was parked within easy reach. She went over to him and took both his hands in hers.

"Hello, Dad."

He smiled up at her. "I was looking forward to this evening. I'm sorry I wasn't more alert the last time you came, but with this cancer, some days are better than others. The spell in hospital helped and the dialysis too. I usually get a few good days afterwards. This is one of those."

He looked gaunt, his hair almost all gone, and the skin

of his face drawn tightly over his forehead and cheekbones. Despite seeing him a week earlier, Isobel still carried with her an image of a robust man — the one who said goodbye to her when she left Toronto for the last time. Looking at him now, she wanted to lean her head on his shoulder and cry like she used to as a child. The time she fell off her first bicycle onto a gravel path and cut open her knee, he had held her close and whispered strange soothing words into her hair. The scar was still there to remind her that, once upon a time, such a small gesture could cure all the problems in her life.

"What brings you to New Zealand? You didn't let us know you were coming to visit."

"Didn't Mom tell you? I explained it to her when I was here last week."

He gave a small laugh. "She might have told me, but like I say, I wasn't at my best. Tell me again."

Even though she had practiced this conversation over the past few days, Isobel hadn't managed to find an easy entrée. Forthright and blunt had been her initial idea, but now she shied away from that approach. She took a chair from the dining table and placed it in front of her father so she could see his face.

"This may be the last chance I get to see you..." Her voice started to crack, and she swallowed hard.

"It's okay Isobel." He reached out and put his hand over hers. "You're right. I know I'm very sick."

"Yeah. Mom told me." She looked down at her hands, unsure how to navigate her way into the conversation she so desperately needed. She lifted her eyes to his. His gaze was steady as if he knew what she was about to say. She took a deep breath and began.

"I never imagined I'd be here like this with you. All the

while we were in Canada, I wanted to ask you about the past, but...but you and Mom didn't want to say anything. Then you left and..." She gave a shrug. "It didn't seem like you wanted me in your lives."

A look of sadness crossed his face. She decided to forge ahead.

"The thing is, Dad, you've never told me how you came to adopt me." She paused, choosing her words carefully. "It's hard to grow up feeling that you've been abandoned by your biological parents. I know I had you and Mom, but at a certain point I had to face the reality that my biological parents gave me away. I need to know why."

Tears were streaming down her face, and she pulled her hand away to wipe them.

"It all came to a head last year. I was working for this Irish lady, Maggie O'Connor, when she told me she got pregnant as a young woman. She had just emigrated to the United States. She couldn't face going back to her parents in Ireland, so she gave the baby up for adoption. She kept that secret for fifty years until she told me. I think it helped, getting it off her chest. It's a long story, but in the end, I found her daughter for her and they reconnected."

"How did it go?"

Isobel was surprised at her father's question.

"Actually, not very well. They both wanted the meeting to happen. Lara, that's the name she gave her daughter, lives in Massachusetts. She's called Grace Mangan now. She flew to Wisconsin to meet Maggie, and I picked her up at the airport and drove her to her hotel. She asked a lot of questions about Maggie. They had arranged to meet for lunch in Madison the following day, just the two of them. When Maggie came home that afternoon she didn't say much. I forgot to tell you I rent

Maggie's guest cottage, so I see her almost every day. It was only later, when she was close to the end — she had cancer too — that she told me she and her daughter didn't see the world the same way. To be honest, I'm not sure Maggie liked her." The disappointment in Isobel's tone was clear.

"That's the problem with full disclosure; it doesn't always work out the way you think. Happy endings are hard to come by." Her father gave her a brief smile. "Let's have dinner, and we'll talk some more afterwards."

Isobel wasn't sure if her mother had been listening. Christina chose that moment to come into the room and offer them both a glass of wine. Her father declined.

"Sadly, it tastes foul to me these days. Just water, thanks," he said, looking to his wife.

He took a sip of water from the lightweight plastic glass she offered him. His hands had a noticeable tremor as he maneuvered the straw to his lips, and looking down at his wrists, Isobel saw how thin they had become.

Isobel's father had always been the keeper of the secret. She was fairly certain her mother knew some of the details, but in the past when she had begged her mother for information, Christina would always look to her father as if for permission. That made it even more critical that Isobel get answers this evening. If her father should die suddenly, she doubted her mother would be willing to go against his wishes, even in death.

The meal reminded Isobel of Sunday dinners in Toronto while she was still at high school. Apple tart was a specialty of her mother's, the pastry made with lard, just as it had been when she was growing up on a farm in New Zealand. She insisted lard made the best pastry, and while Isobel herself would never use lard, she had to admit that in this her mother was right.

Describing her adventure on the Abel Tasman Coastal Trail was a perfect distraction during the meal. Isobel was a good raconteur and had both of her parents laughing as she gave an account of her initial meeting with Stan.

"She's a fantastic guide, though she scares me a bit. Still, I'd definitely trust her with my life."

When dinner was finished, Isobel helped her mother clear away the dishes.

While they were in the kitchen together, Christina said, "You need to go back in to your father," a note of urgency in her voice. "Take advantage of this opportunity. He's willing to talk, and he needs to get this off his chest before..." Her voice cracked.

"You should be there too, Mom. You're part of it."

They went back into the sitting room together. Isobel's father had moved his wheelchair from the dining table and was now facing the sofa. The two women sat down, the space between them wide enough to reflect their years of separation, but at least it was not a chasm.

CHAPTER 17

The silence was palpable. Isobel could hear the tick of a clock somewhere in the house. Her father was looking down at his hands and for a moment Isobel wondered if he would disappoint her once again. Then she heard an intake of breath. He looked up, his eyes fixing on hers.

"I think the most important thing for you to know is that you are my brother's daughter. He asked me to take care of you, and I did. *We* did." He looked towards his wife and gave her a gentle smile.

"The reason we never told you is complex, but when I finish, you'll understand why. It would have been a burden, especially when you were young. My silence protected me as well as you. The Bosnian war ended in a peace of sorts, but grudges and vendettas never end."

Isobel could see the effort her father was making, each word delivered slowly and with frequent pauses as he struggled to catch his breath. He looked towards Christina again.

"Your mother wanted me to tell you everything before we left Canada, but I was afraid... selfish too. I did not understand how damaging that decision was for you." He shook his head wearily. "I'm so sorry, Isobel."

Reaching a trembling hand towards her, he touched her hand lightly. She covered it with her own, holding the frail offering.

"My brother Tomislav — we called him Toma — was ten years younger than me. Even though we were both born in Yugoslavia while it was still one country, we grew up in different worlds. Yugoslavia was falling apart, and we all knew that the end would be bloody."

Her father sighed deeply and in that sigh Isobel heard the echo of his loss. Not once in her life had she ever considered what it must have cost him to emigrate.

"I left Yugoslavia before things got really bad. But Toma was different."

He made a sound in his throat that might have been a laugh. Isobel wasn't sure.

"Did you know the name Toma means ruler? Even when we were children, my brother always wanted to be the boss. The war gave him his chance...becoming someone big and important in the new state. Greater Serbia." He scoffed as he uttered the name, his voice taking on a derisory note. "Toma and I were not even born in Serbia. We were Serbians all right, but we were born in Bosnia."

Withdrawing his hand from hers, her father reached for his glass. Christina stood up and went to help him. After he took a sip of water, she hovered behind his chair, clearly disturbed by the effort her husband was making.

"Do you know anything about the Bosnian war?" he asked.

"Not much," Isobel admitted. "I mean, I know some terrible things happened. I've heard about Srebrenica."

"Ah yes. Srebrenica. That horror finally made the world

wake up. Before that nobody cared about Yugoslavia or what it had become." There was bitterness in his tone.

"Serbs living in Bosnia became second-class citizens. Money, jobs, housing, building contracts...they all went to Bosnians. Toma was not the only angry young man at that time. There were many who believed in a Greater Serbia and were willing to fight for it."

Isobel's mother interrupted briefly, asking if she would like tea, but she declined. She could see her father was exhausted but desperately wanted him to continue, worried that if he stopped now this confession might be lost forever. When he spoke next, his tone was lighter and there was a hint of a smile.

"Your father was very good-looking and popular. He could have had any girl he wanted in Serbia."

Isobel leaned forward slightly at the mention of her father.

"Unfortunately, he fell in love with a Bosnian girl called Amela."

Isobel gave a sharp intake of breath.

"That was my mother's name?"

"Yes. Amela. It's a Slavic name. It means hope."

He shifted his position in the wheelchair as if it might help him take a deeper breath. The oxygen machine clicked. Isobel waited, her body tense.

"Toma and I had chosen different paths by then. We disagreed that there could ever be a political solution in the country." The corners of his mouth turned down abruptly. "We stopped speaking."

Standing behind her husband's chair, Christina rested her hands on his frail shoulders. Isobel could feel that the story was coming to the end.

"I was living in Canada then. I had a good life with Christina. Toma and I had lost contact. I had no idea what he was doing or what his involvement in the war was. Then one day he called. I couldn't believe it was him on the phone after all those years. He asked for a favor from his 'big brother.' He used those exact words, *veliki brat*. He told me he had married a Bosnian girl from Sarajevo and that they had a daughter. His wife had been killed in a bombing a few days earlier. I remember that moment because he began to sob. He said he needed to get his daughter out of the city, that she would be a target. He had many enemies, he said, and they would try to kidnap or kill her. Then he asked me if I would take you."

Isobel's father looked directly at her, and she saw pride and love in his eyes. In the silence that followed, she could almost hear their two hearts beating, hers rapidly, her father's deathly slow. It took her every ounce of self-control to wait for him to get his breath back.

"A woman called Gordana brought you to Canada. She was a friend of your mother's, I think. I don't know how Toma arranged it. He must have had friends, powerful friends. Bribes? Threats? Who knows?" He gave a shrug. "You came with official-looking papers, but I'm sure they were forged. Even so, the Canadian authorities accepted them and...we adopted you."

Closing his eyes, her father sank back into the wheelchair. He looked as if all the life force had been squeezed from his body. Minutes passed before he gathered sufficient strength to finish the narrative.

"I was sure Toma would contact us after the war ended and take you back to Serbia. You were five by then." He gave Isobel a weak smile, as if he were seeing that little girl. "I knew some people in Bosnia still, so I made inquiries. They told me Toma had died in the war."

Time stood still for Isobel in that moment. For the first time in her life, she had no questions. Her anger and resentment had dissipated, replaced by something approaching admiration. In her mind she saw a little five-year-old girl, an orphan, the collateral damage of war.

With a shaking hand her father reached for his water. Isobel could see his throat muscles contracting as he swallowed each careful sip. The water seemed to give him renewed strength, and he straightened in his wheelchair, preparing to say something more.

"I know we were not the parents you wanted, but we took our responsibility seriously. We made sure you were safe, got a good education, medical care...all those things."

His voice rose, sounding almost plaintive to Isobel.

"Neither your mother nor I ever wanted to have children." He paused to let this sink in. "It was something we agreed on long before you came into our lives. We wanted our freedom. Perhaps now you can understand why it was hard for us. Christina had to give up her job. We didn't have a lot of money. What I'm trying to say is, it wasn't easy for us either."

Her father's eyes were moist with tears. Her mother came around to the front of his wheelchair and bent over him, wrapping her arms around his frail frame. She kissed his cheek.

"I think it's time for you to go now," she said to Isobel in a quiet voice. "Your father needs to rest."

"Can I come back tomorrow? Please?"

"Let's see how your father is feeling tomorrow. I'll call you in the morning."

Chapter 18

At last she knew the truth. She was not a war baby. She'd had a father called Toma and a mother called Amela. They had loved each other. Had there not been a war she would have grown up with them. Above all, she had *not* been abandoned. All those years of wasted emotion, anger and resentment, had drained away, leaving her feeling strangely empty. He father's words were still ringing in her ears when she pulled the car over to the side of the road. "He was good-looking and popular, and he could have had any girl he wanted." She rested her forehead on the steering wheel and sobbed as if her heart could break.

There was no point in trying to call Vic. He'd be fast asleep now. Besides, a phone ringing in the middle of the night usually meant bad news. Nor had she the emotional energy to talk to him. Before she could share what she had just discovered, she needed time to process it herself. Inevitably, he would ask when she was going to come home. But for some reason Isobel didn't quite understand, the idea of going home now, of settling back into her old life, didn't have the urgency it had a few days ago. She needed time to adjust to this new version of Isobel.

The prospect of spending the rest of the evening alone in her hotel room was dismal. She drove into town and parked opposite Stan's Place, not quite sure what she wanted. A friendly face? A sympathetic ear? Stan wasn't the sort of person who hugged, but she was a good listener. Perhaps she would still be at work and could be persuaded to go to the pub across the street.

A "closed" sign was propped up in the display window of the store, but Isobel rapped on the door. Just as she was about to give up and leave, out of the corner of her eye she saw a movement in the back of the store. Then Stan's face appeared, looking as if she was about to berate whomever had disturbed her evening. Seeing Isobel, her frown relaxed. She unlocked the door and poked her head out.

"I thought you'd be long gone by now. Weren't you going to see your folks and have it out with them?"

"Yeah, I did." Isobel's voice was flat.

"So....? What did they say?" Stan's eyes widened.

"Guess what? My dad is really my uncle."

"Were you surprised?"

"Why do you say that?" Isobel's voice had a sharp edge to it.

"Well, after you told me this couple adopted you out of the blue, and they didn't seem that keen on having a kid, it seemed pretty obvious they couldn't refuse to take you. You told me you were born in Sarajevo. That's where your dad is from, isn't it? So, considering your mother is a Kiwi, it had to be something to do with him." She tapped the side of her head dramatically. "It's not quite Sherlock Holmes, luvvy."

"I suppose...I just.... He should have told me long ago. It would have changed everything." The corners of her mouth quivered. "That's not all. My real parents are both dead."

Tears welled up in her eyes and spilled down her cheeks. She wiped them away with the back of her hand.

"Ah, luvvy. That's a tough one. You'd always hoped, hadn't you?"

Stan opened the door wide and stepped outside. "C'mon," she said, taking Isobel by the arm. "Let's go to the pub. You need a drink."

∽

They sat at a table in a quiet corner where none of the patrons, some of whom nodded to Stan as she entered, were likely to disturb them. Isobel repeated every detail of her father's conversation. Occasionally Stan interrupted, but she didn't mind. The story was acquiring form and substance in the telling. She could almost see her mother and father, Toma and Amela, and later a woman walking purposefully towards an airplane, a baby in her arms.

"Sounds like a scene from Casablanca, if you ask me," said Stan when she heard about Gordana's role.

Isobel couldn't help grinning. "I think the plane was probably bigger. I hope I wasn't crying for the whole journey."

Stan's expression was thoughtful. "I have to feel a bit sorry for your mum, even if you don't like her much. I mean, she got a bit of a raw deal, didn't she?"

"Yeah. I suppose she did. It's funny how you see things one way, then all of a sudden they get turned around."

"Couldn't get rid of you, could they? A bit like a stray cat you put a saucer of milk out for." Stan shook her head knowingly. "Been there, done that...though the cat moved on." She gave a guffaw. "The neighbor lady gave it fish."

Isobel found herself smiling. Stan looked over the rim of

her beer at Isobel, who was cupping a glass of white wine in her hands. Her voice had become serious.

"What are you going to do now?"

"I don't honestly know. I suppose the easiest thing would be to just go home. After all, I found out what I came for."

Stan nodded. She took another sip of beer and waited for Isobel to continue.

"There's still a bunch of questions I want to ask."

"Like what?" Stan's eyebrows jumped upward. "I mean, if you could only ask one, what would be the most important question right now?"

"Mmm." Isobel pursed her lips. "I can't pick one; there's too many. For example, does he know how my parents met? Does he have any photos of his brother from when they were kids? Was Toma good at sports?"

Isobel's voice rose as she enumerated each question on her fingers. Suddenly, she banged her fists on the table.

"I know they sound stupid, but I want to know everything… everything he remembers. If I leave now, that'll be the end of it. He'll die, and I'll never find out anything more."

"So, stay." Stan's statement sounded like a command.

Isobel shook her head. "I can't stay here forever. And I can't stay with them — my dad's too sick and my mom is way too stressed out."

"Stay with me then. I've got a room you can have for a couple of weeks at least. After that I've got another guiding trip lined up, although you could stay there without me. I don't think you'll burn the place down or run away with the silver."

Isobel looked at Stan, not sure whether the offer was genuine.

Stan let out a laugh. "I'm not *that* scary, am I?"

Isobel smiled weakly. "It's a really kind offer."

"Not everyone would agree with you, luvvy." She rolled her eyes and made a gesture towards the bar man.

Her voice softened. "Why don't you move your things from that fancy hotel of yours to my place tomorrow? It'll give you a bit more time to spend with your dad, see what happens."

Too exhausted to come up with another plan, Isobel nodded her agreement. "Okay. I give in. Thank you so much. Where do you live anyway?"

"Where do you think? Stan's Place."

Chapter 19

Isobel felt a little uncomfortable as she drove to Stan's Place the following morning. After all, the offer of accommodation had been made late the previous evening after Stan had consumed several beers and a whiskey nightcap. Isobel had been more restrained but had to admit she should not have been driving a rental car back to her hotel, especially in the dark. Fortunately, everyone in Kaiteriteri seemed to be in bed by the time she left the pub.

Driving down the winding hill that led into town, Isobel tried to assemble the shreds of a dream from the night before. In it she was staying in an unfamiliar house, but when she tried to leave, she couldn't find any door leading to the outside. Moving from room to room, she had looked out each of the windows in turn, but nothing in the view was familiar. She hadn't felt trapped, just lost and unsure what to do next. The dream had ended abruptly when she heard the door of the room next to hers bang noisily as the occupants left, presumably going to the dining room for breakfast. She checked her phone, but as yet there was no message from her mother. Soon afterwards she followed the other guests and sat at a window table to admire the view one last time. For a few minutes she considered calling Stan to say she had changed her mind. But no matter how lovely the hotel was, every time she returned to her room, she was overcome by an intense feeling of isolation.

After breakfast and with some reluctance, she called Vic on their home phone. She didn't want to tell him her biological parents were dead, didn't want to say those words aloud. He would have questions for which she had no answers. She'd listen to the sympathy in his voice and start crying again. Instead, she decided to tell him she was "making progress," that her father couldn't talk for long at a time, and that she would see her father again today or tomorrow. It wasn't a complete lie but nor was it the truth. She decided she could live with it. The phone rang several times before switching to the machine, where she left her message.

∼

Anyone driving along the waterfront in Kaiteriteri couldn't help but notice the colorful sign attached to a tall wooden fence announcing Stan's Place, with an arrow pointing around the corner to the storefront and the parking lot. The fence partially hid the back of the building from the street.

Isobel parked in the gravel lot and left her luggage in the car; she didn't want to appear presumptuous, in case Stan had changed her mind. As she walked towards the building this time, she scrutinized it more carefully. Situated a block from the waterfront on a corner lot, the two-story structure was sided in darkly stained wood, giving it a rustic appearance. Like most of the buildings in town, Stan's Place had a tin roof. Two single-story extensions projected from the back of the building, bracketing a small garden.

"Stan?" Isobel called out tentatively, as she opened the door and entered the store, expecting to see a head of spiky pink and green hair emerge from somewhere in the back.

Instead, a young man sat behind the counter reading a book. He looked up at her and grinned. She was immediately struck by his features, which showed an attractive blend of Maori and European influences. Almond-shaped brown eyes and dark eyebrows, slightly too-long curly hair, perfect white teeth that contrasted with his day-old shadow. For a moment she stared at him, quite forgetting why she had come into the store. With a slight tilt of his head, he broke the spell and Isobel regained her composure.

"Is Stan around? I think she was expecting me."

"*Kia ora*. You must be Isobel. She said you'd be coming by sometime today."

He walked out from behind the counter and held out his hand. He was about five foot ten, slightly built, with the easy movements of someone accustomed to sports. A faded maroon hoodie, black T-shirt, blue jeans, and battered-looking sneakers made it clear that he didn't feel the need to dress for work.

"I'm Kauri, Stan's nephew. She'll be back later this afternoon. She had to go into Nelson."

"Oh, well...I'll come back later, then."

"Nah. Don't go away. She said you were coming to stay and to show you where you'd be sleeping." Seeing no luggage he said, "I can help you with your things if you like."

Isobel surprised herself by agreeing to his offer. He held the door open for her and followed her to her car. Then, with practiced ease he slung her daypack over his shoulder and grabbed the handle of her carry-on. She followed him back into the store, past the racks of clothing and outdoor gear, through a storeroom lined with stacked cardboard boxes, and finally through another door into a large room that clearly served as the hub of Stan's living space. A long narrow island divided the kitchen from the living space. Against one wall stood a wood-burning stove and facing it, an L-shaped leather sofa. The walls were covered in paintings and weavings, and every surface had something on it that drew the eye, warranting further investigation. Through a pair of large windows on the back wall of the room, she could see a garden surrounded by a wooden fence, presumably the same one she had seen a few minutes earlier with the sign for Stan's Place.

Kauri continued through a door on the left, again holding it open for Isobel. They entered a narrow hallway.

"I'm sure she means you to sleep here," he said, opening another door, "And that's the bathroom directly opposite. Sorry, but you'll have to share it with whichever of us is working in the store. It's the only one on the ground floor. Stan has her own upstairs."

Isobel looked around, recognizing this as one of the single-story additions she had seen from the outside. The room had its own entrance, with a line of steppingstones leading across the garden to a gate in the fence.

"Stan said to make yourself at home, get a cup of tea, check out the fridge, that sort of thing. I'll be in the shop if you need anything or have any questions. Okay?"

Dropping her bags on the wooden floor, Kauri gave her another one of his radiant smiles. She searched for something to say that might prolong the moment but couldn't think of anything. Instead, she muttered a thank you. He left, closing the door quietly behind him.

Isobel took stock of her new quarters. The contrast with her hotel room could not have been greater. Here the furnishings and décor were minimal and basic. She sat on the edge of the double bed and bounced a couple of times, testing it for firmness. Pleased to find it was as good as the one she had slept in the previous night, although by no means as large, she inspected the wardrobe and chest of drawers. The former held extra pillows and a couple of blankets, and enough hangers to satisfy the most sartorial of guests. All of the drawers were empty and spotlessly clean. She almost expected to find a bible in the bottom drawer of the dresser but reminded herself that this was New Zealand, not the United States. The thought of Stan issuing bibles to unsuspecting guests prompted a laugh, which she quickly stifled, hoping that Kauri had not heard. More than anything the room had a pleasant, lived-in feeling. Loneliness might be less acute here.

Unclear as to what time her mother might call, Isobel decided to walk around Kaiteriteri. The town was small with barely 300 inhabitants, according to a brochure she had picked up at the hotel, although the population increased significantly during the summer months. At this time of year when temperatures barely reached sixty degrees, no kayakers nor paddleboarders braved the sea, despite the inviting turquoise waters of the bay. The brochure also described a popular hike along the coastline south of town, but she wasn't sure if the trail would be within range of cell service.

Her phone rang while she was having a coffee at the Beached Whale, which was fast becoming her go-to place. Her bona fides had been established the previous evening by drinking with Stan, and this time she was greeted by name. She had learned to substitute her usual order of coffee with a splash of cream by asking for a flat white, and the resulting mix, somewhere between a latte and a cappuccino, was beginning to grow on her.

"We're at the hospital in Nelson right now," her mother

said without preamble. "He wasn't feeling well this morning, so I drove him here. They're keeping him overnight, so there's no point in you coming to the house today."

It felt like a dismissal, and Isobel wondered if her mother hated her for having disrupted their quiet lives in Motueka. Had she not appeared on their doorstep a week earlier, maybe they would have muddled along until her father's disease eventually caught up with him. Her father. Isobel's brain stumbled over the word. It was going to take some time to adjust to the fact that he was her uncle. By then he might be dead. Two dead fathers. A sigh of despair escaped her, which her mother must have heard.

"You could visit him tomorrow, I suppose. Best to call the hospital first. He's in room 314. I'm going back there now to sit with him a while. I'll talk to you later."

Before Isobel had a chance to say anything more, the line went dead. She sat a while longer, sipping at her coffee, which was now lukewarm, and thought about her mother. She struggled to recall a time when her mother had said "I love you." Once, when she fell from a swing in the neighbor's garden, her mother had soothed her crying by giving her a cup of tea with lots of sugar and milk — no substitute for the hug she had yearned for.

The screen on Isobel's phone showed 4:15, too late to go for a hike. Stan would surely be back from Nelson by now. Perhaps she would offer to cook dinner, especially if her nephew was there. Cheered by that thought, Isobel returned to Stan's Place, entering by the shop instead of the garden, and making a mental note to ask about a key. The shop was deserted, so she walked through it to the kitchen. She was looking forward to seeing the crusty woman again. Instead, she found Kauri sprawled out on the couch, his head buried in the same book as earlier. Her heart gave a little jolt.

"Been a quiet day," he announced, holding the book up for her to see. "I'm nearly finished."

It took a moment for Isobel to get her head around his accent, which was much stronger than Stan's.

"What's the book?" she asked, walking over to where he was sitting.

He turned it over to show her the cover. Three hands, their fingers outstretched, reached towards each other against a backdrop of what might be a moon or a watery sun. She read the title, *The Bone People*.

"It's by a Kiwi, Keri Hulme. She won a prize for it, although that was years ago. It's really good." He nodded his head enthusiastically. "You can have it when I'm finished, if you like."

Isobel smiled, not sure if he was just making conversation or if the offer was genuine.

"By the way, Stan called. She said to tell you she won't be back from Nelson this evening."

In Isobel's mind, the words "Nelson" and "hospital" had become inexorably linked.

"Anything wrong?" she asked, her voice rising slightly.

"Nah. She often stays over. Her friend Meg lives there."

He got up from the sofa and walked towards the kitchen.

"She said to cook dinner for you, so I hope you eat curry. I'm not much good at anything else. Is chicken okay? I can leave it out if you prefer."

He gave her another of his dazzling smiles, and she realized that no matter what he offered, she would agree to it.

"Chicken is great," she said. "I can hop over to the bar and get a bottle of wine, or beer, if you prefer?"

"I drink anything." His eyes twinkled.

For the third time in less than twenty-four hours, Isobel found herself walking into the Beached Whale. When he saw her, the barman laughed out loud. He opened his mouth to make a comment, but she deflected it by asking for a bottle of wine and a six-pack of beer.

"You and Stan going to get munted then?" He gave a chuckle.

It was a word she had never heard before, but she had a good idea what it meant. She blushed.

"No. Just making sure everyone has what they like. The thing is, I don't know anything about wines, or beers for that matter. You pick out a wine that'll work with a chicken curry and whatever beer Stan normally drinks."

The barman nodded and returned a few minutes later with a bottle of Marlborough Sauvignon Blanc and a six pack of beer.

"The Sav should work just fine with the curry. As for the beer, Stan's not picky. She was drinking Speights last night."

Isobel paid and put the chilled bottles in a bag she had picked up on her way out of the house. By the time she returned, Kauri was busily chopping onions. Every so often the rice cooker on the counter emitted a gentle puff of steam, adding to the already interesting aroma.

"Can I do anything?" she asked, as she watched him move efficiently from counter to stove to fridge to sink, reshaping his work triangle into a square.

"Speights? Great. Can you pop the top off one of those beauties for me. This is hard work, you know."

His eyes crinkled up as he gave her another immaculate smile. How did he get such perfect teeth, she wondered. Did they come with being Maori? As a child she had endured years of braces, hating every minute of the ordeal. Still, she had perfectly straight teeth now and was thankful for her mother's insistence at the time. Her mother. Reluctantly, Isobel acknowledged that in some ways Christina *had* tried.

She opened the beer and handed it to Kauri, who paused from chopping to take a swig.

"What about you?" he asked.

"I'm a wine drinker," she admitted, "and I like your Sauvignon Blancs. They're very different from what we get in the States. I don't drink it there, but here it tastes perfect."

She continued to watch him, savoring the aromatic smell coming from a pan on the stove. She found herself salivating and realized she was extremely hungry.

"How's the wine?" he asked, turning from the stove where he was now stirring the contents of a large pot.

"It's good. Do you want to try some?"

"Nah. I'll stick to beer for now. Maybe after dinner."

"Might not be much left by then. It's been a rough couple of days." She made a wry face.

"Want to talk about it?"

When she didn't answer, he returned to work, accepting her silence with equanimity. Earlier she had set the table, following his directions as to where to find plates and cutlery. Now, she sat on one of the two chairs that faced each other across the small oblong table. A few minutes later he brought the bowls of curry and rice to the table, setting them down with an elaborate flourish.

"Madam," he said jokingly, "your dinner is served." They both laughed, recognizing the incongruity of the situation. Yet Isobel didn't feel the slightest bit uncomfortable with this man. They ate the first few bites in silence, each savoring the complex mixture of exotic spices.

Looking up from her plate, she said, "This is so kind of you…to cook dinner for me, I mean. And it's really good."

"I'm glad you like it. I enjoy cooking, especially when it's not just for myself."

They chatted easily over the meal, the conversation ranging widely from wine and food to travel and politics. Kauri had left New Zealand after high school and spent several years in Australia, working a variety of jobs.

"In the end I missed New Zealand. I suppose to most Americans there's not much difference between the two countries. We come from the same region in the southern hemisphere and speak the same language, sort of. But Australia never felt like home. And then there's my family, my *whanau*. They're here."

"I get it. It's a bit like Canada and the States, with Canada the junior partner. People here assume I'm American."

"Yeah. But your mum's from New Zealand, isn't she? At least that's what Stan told me."

Kauri's open expression begged a response. Isobel thought about deflecting his question, then reconsidered. She wanted to talk, as if by doing so she might rid herself of the conflicting emotions that seemed to increase with every day. Much as she would have liked to erase them, her father's words from the previous evening were seared into her brain. "We did the best we could." Her parents hadn't chosen her. They were forced. Well, maybe not forced, but certainly coerced. It was a request her father couldn't refuse, and her mother was compelled to play a role she never wanted. It explained so much.

She took a deep breath and began, telling him about Maggie and how she had left Isobel enough money to try and find her biological parents, or at least find out why they had given her up for adoption. By the time she finished, tears were streaming down her face, and her shoulders were heaving.

Kauri reached his hand across the table to take hers. She grabbed it and squeezed hard as if the effort could quell her suppressed sobs.

"Would a hug help?"

Isobel nodded. She came around to his side of the table and leaned her head on his shoulder. He patted her back tentatively, then maneuvered her to sit on his lap, wrapping his arms around her. She relaxed into his embrace, closing her eyes and listening to the reassuring sound of his heartbeat. After a few minutes they moved to the sofa where they lay together. Kauri stroked her hair, murmuring soothingly as she buried her face in his chest. His words worked a magic of sorts, allowing her anguish to dissipate, only to be replaced by a feeling of recklessness. Removed from any reminder of her previous twenty-seven years, she felt an urgent desire to be loved by this man. She began to shiver, not sure whether it was from the situation or the evening chill. Sensing it, Kauri released her and got up from the sofa.

"Wrap this around you," he said, offering her a woolen blanket that was draped over the back of the sofa. "Give me a few minutes, and I'll get a fire going."

After the softness of his chest, the blanket felt coarse against her bare neck. She watched as he squatted in front of the stove, expertly arranging paper and sticks and larger pieces of wood. He lit the paper and closed the glass-fronted door, leaving a tiny opening for the fire to draw. She heard the initial whoosh followed by a crackling sound as the sticks caught, then a deeper steady purr as the logs began to burn. He closed the door to the stove fully and turned to face her. She held her breath. She knew exactly what she wanted to happen, knew instinctively that she wanted to fold herself into his arms again, make love with him, and lose herself. He seemed to know it too.

Chapter 20

Sometime in the middle of the night, when the fire had died down, they moved to Isobel's room. Even though Kauri had assured her that Stan rarely came back early after spending the night with her lover in Nelson, Isobel didn't want to risk the embarrassment. She could imagine the ribald comments Stan would inevitably make on finding her and Kauri on the couch wrapped around each other.

He was everything she hoped for in a lover, careful to make sure this was what she truly wanted, gentle yet assertive, and anxious to pleasure her. She had enjoyed every moment of their night together. Waking the following morning, she studied his face. Even in sleep, his eyes and mouth seemed to be smiling. She smiled back at him, grateful that he had helped her step away from her life, if only for a night.

Kauri stirred. An image of Vic flashed into her mind, but she pushed the thought aside. It would only lead to guilt and smother the warm pulse of joy she could feel in her groin. Her hand went to her clitoris. Kauri moved closer, his hand gently pushing hers aside. They made love again, this time more urgently, as if they were going to be interrupted at any minute.

Reluctantly Isobel withdrew from his embrace and pushed the covers aside.

"We'd better clean up the kitchen before Stan gets back," she said, acknowledging the reality of the day that lay ahead.

"And I'd better open up the shop. I didn't leave a note on the door. That's what Stan does when she's going to be away."

Grinning from ear to ear, he tried to pull her to him again, but she pushed him away.

"I don't want to be responsible for you losing your job," she said with a laugh.

"Not a chance," he replied. "Stan's my *whanau*, my family. She can't get rid of me."

~

Soon after they parted company, Isobel called the hospital to inquire about her father. She was surprised when they put her through to his room and he picked up the phone.

"Hi, Dad. It's Isobel. Mom told me you were at the hospital. How are you?"

The words sounded formulaic, even to her ears, and she wished she had prefaced them with telling him she had been worried. But she hadn't worried about him, at least not last night.

"I'm okay, not much worse than usual. I gave your mother a bit of a scare. Still, the doctors seem to think it was a good idea to bring me here. They're keeping me for a few days. It'll be good for your mother to get a bit of a break. This way, she won't have to worry about me."

"Are they allowing you to have visitors?"

"They haven't told me otherwise, so I suppose so."

"Then, if it's okay, I'll come to see you later today."

"That would be nice. There's not much to do here besides watch television, and you know I was never one for doing that, unless it's soccer." He gave a little laugh.

"Okay, Dad, I'll see you later."

~

Isobel considered stopping in Motueka to see if her mother wanted to come along with her but dismissed the thought. She didn't want to be alone with her mother right now. Their relationship was changing gradually. Nonetheless, there were childhood memories that needed to be reanalyzed before they could be reshaped, or perhaps even dismissed. It would take time. Her relationship with her father was, of necessity, changing rapidly. Thinking about him now, knowing he was never going to get better, she felt a stab of anguish. She would miss him when he was gone. A wave of sadness engulfed her. She could have tried harder. But she had been so angry.

For the remainder of the drive to the hospital, Isobel thought about what she most wanted to ask her father. There were still so many questions and the ever-present worry that they would run out of time. "What was my father like? Did he look like you? Did you ever meet my mother? Do you know if my grandparents are still alive? Do they live in Bosnia or Serbia? Do I have any other relatives?" The list grew longer and longer so that by the time she arrived, she wasn't sure which she would bring up first.

The lady at the reception desk directed Isobel to the third floor. Walking up the stairs, she realized her mother might also be there. She hoped that wasn't the case. Her father's answers might be constrained if her mother was present, and she herself might feel reluctant to broach certain topics.

Room 314 had two beds, but only one was occupied. Her father's eyes were closed. He seemed to have become even more shrunken, with a pallor that almost matched the pillows against which his feeble frame rested. An intravenous stand hovered by the side of his bed, a line of plastic tubing winding its way to his hand, which rested listlessly on the bed covering. The ever-present nasal cannulas clung to his sunken cheeks.

Silently, Isobel lifted a chair propped against the wall and placed it beside the bed. She sat down and looked at her father's face, trying to see the younger, healthier man who was there throughout her childhood. Were his eyes blue or brown? It came as a shock to realize she didn't know. Her father opened them suddenly, and she saw that his eyes were brown.

"Have you been sitting here long?" he asked, shifting slightly to sit up.

"I just got here. I'm sorry if I woke you."

He started to speak but almost immediately began to cough. As he reached for the glass of water on the bedside table, Isobel jumped up to get it for him, placing it in his hand and orienting the straw towards his mouth. Despite his tremor, he managed to return the glass to the table without spilling it.

"It must have been a shock for you the other evening. I'm so sorry. I should have told you a long time ago." He gave a sigh, "But after a while there didn't seem to be any point. The truth could only hurt you, or at least that's what I thought. Stupid. Stupid."

He shut his eyes for a moment, as if he was gathering strength.

"Honestly, I'm fine," Isobel said, trying to sound reassuring. "It's not as if I didn't have a mom and a dad. I mean I wasn't brought up in an orphanage or anything. You were good parents. You looked after me well. It couldn't have been easy for the two of you, especially Mom."

Listening to these words, Isobel realized she was no longer using them as platitudes. Something had shifted — a breach in the resentment she had carried for so many years.

"Funny, but I can't switch to thinking of you as my uncle. I guess you'll always be Dad."

Her father smiled, then reached for her hand. She touched his fingers, careful to avoid the intravenous line. They talked for the next hour, during which Isobel listened to the story of her father's early life in a small town in Bosnia. At times he closed his eyes, his face relaxed as if he were seeing his childhood again. Isobel listened as if in a trance, seeing not just her dad but her real father in these vignettes. Toma was coming to life, if only in her imagination.

"Toma was born in 1967. I was ten at the time. Yugoslavia was pretty stable then. Officially, it was called the Socialist Federal Republic of Yugoslavia and consisted of six republics, a bit like the Provinces in Canada, with Josip Broz Tito as its president. Everyone called him Tito. We came from Bosnia, and then there was Croatia, Montenegro, Macedonia, Slovenia, and of course, Serbia. Some of the republics were dominated by an ethnic group, a bit like French Canadians in Quebec. In Bosnia the ethnic groups were Croats, Serbs, and Bosniaks. Religion was important to some people even though Yugoslavia was a socialist country. In the town where we grew up there were Muslims, Catholics, and Orthodox Christians. Our parents weren't religious, and as kids we didn't care. It was only later things changed, that it mattered what religion you were or what ethnic group you came from."

His voice was becoming weaker, and he stopped talking for a few minutes to recharge his lungs with the enriched air.

"Of course, everything is different now thanks to tourism."

"I'd like to go there some time," Isobel said, giving him a chance to pause and rest. Even as she said it, she realized she did indeed have a strong desire to see where her biological parents were born and grew up.

"What was Toma like? I know you disagreed over politics. But when you were kids, did you get on well?"

She leaned forward a little, not wanting to miss a word.

"I loved having a little brother," he said, the corners of his mouth lifting.

Before he could continue, the door opened and a nurse entered the room. With a cursory nod to Isobel, she checked the bag of fluid hanging from the stand, then exchanged it for a full one. The nurse checked her father's pulse and raised him up slightly in the bed, fluffing the pillows behind him. No sooner had she left than an orderly came in with a lunch tray. The mood had been broken, and until her father finished his meal, Isobel was resigned to waiting. He ate slowly, chewing and swallowing each mouthful laboriously and sipping from his water glass in between bites. During this time, he didn't look at her, and she wondered if he was composing what he might say when he had finished eating.

Then her mother arrived.

"I didn't know you were going to be here," Christina said, coming into the room and pulling a chair to the opposite side of the bed.

Isobel listened for a note of disapproval in her mother's voice, but there was none.

"I was just about to leave," Isobel said. "I promised Stan I'd be back to help her in the shop this afternoon. She's doing inventory, and it's only fair that I help. After all, she's letting me stay at her house."

The lie was deliberate. She didn't want to impose upon her mother, who she was beginning to see in a completely different light.

"Oh. I didn't realize you had left the hotel," her mother said, clearly surprised. "You know, you could always stay with us...at least until your father comes home from hospital."

"Thanks, Mom, but I know you've set up the house for Dad. No need to change that. I'm fine at Stan's. She's got a guest bedroom with its own entrance. It's kind of like an Airbnb. She and I get along well. She's quite the character."

Her mother hesitated before asking, "Do you want to come over for dinner some evening? Perhaps tomorrow or the day after?"

"Sure, tomorrow would be great," Isobel said.

The expression on her mother's face was difficult to interpret. Apprehension perhaps? Their evolving relationship was going to be challenging for both of them.

"Okay then. I'll see you around six," her mother said, her smile returning when she looked at her husband.

Chapter 21

When Isobel and Kauri parted company that morning, neither of them broached the possibility of their evening together being anything more than a one-night stand. Even so, the way Kauri had looked at her as she dressed and left for the hospital gave her the impression he might want more. For her part, the sense of abandon and recklessness of the previous evening was dissipating and being replaced by a niggling feeling of guilt. A part of her wanted to repeat that blissful escape, while the more rational side of her brain pointed out this was Stan's nephew, and Stan would be returning soon. It would be easier to see him again if she were still at the hotel, but had she not come to stay with Stan, she wouldn't be in this predicament.

Kauri occupied her thoughts for most of the drive back to Kaiteriteri from the hospital. Would he be at Stan's Place or had he gone home, wherever that was? She recognized Stan's car when she drove up to the building; it was flanked by two others. She sat in her car for a couple of minutes, trying to compose herself. On the way back from Nelson, she had made a stop at a liquor store to get more wine and beer for her hostess, dismissing the idea of flowers or chocolates. With a final nod to fate, she got out of the car. She had debated entering by the shop entrance, but in the end opted for the gate leading to the garden where her arrival might not be noticed immediately. Her room was exactly as she had left it, the bed a rumpled mess. If Stan had chanced to look in during the day, she'd know immediately, Isobel thought. She heard voices coming from the living room. Kauri was still here.

"Well, look what the cat dragged in," Stan said when Isobel walked into the kitchen. "A cat that got the cream, it looks like." This was followed by a raucous laugh.

Isobel placed the wine and beer on the kitchen table. She could feel a blush rising to her face and tried to avoid Stan's gaze.

"Looks like you two have met before," Stan said, gesturing to the figure lounging on the couch.

"Come on, Auntie," Kauri said to Stan. "Don't embarrass her. It's not fair." With that, he came over to Isobel and kissed her firmly on the mouth.

Any resolve she might have had disappeared immediately.

"Why don't you open one of those," Stan said, gesturing to the six-pack of beer, "and we can have a drink before dinner. I'm on chef duty for tonight, so no caviar and champagne like last night with Kauri. It's fish on the grill and salad. Good, healthy, local food. I hope it's enough for you two to keep your strength up." She lifted an eyebrow mischievously as she looked from one to the other.

∼

Isobel awoke in the middle of the night. With Kauri deeply asleep beside her, she knew there would be no refuge from the night gremlins. This was the collective name she had given to all the details she had kept from Vic thus far. Finding Maggie close to death and walking away, hiding how much money Maggie transferred into her account, relinquishing her place in vet school and, now, sleeping with Kauri. She felt as if the real Isobel was somewhere else, and the person lying in bed with this beautiful Maori man an imposter. As the night wore on, her regrets gathered strength. She came to a decision. Once she left Kaiteriteri, it would be as if none of this ever happened. She would relegate Kauri to a place in her brain that was firmly closed off. Nonetheless, the interlude at Stan's had shown her what she was capable of. By deviating from her carefully orchestrated life, she had experienced a heady sense of control.

∼

Isobel planned to visit her father that afternoon before going to her mother's house for dinner. With nothing to do for the rest of the morning, she asked Kauri for ideas. He suggested she drive to a popular nearby viewpoint but warned her not to attempt driving up the steep road, which was used to access the communications tower at the top.

"Do you want to come?" she asked, trying not to sound too eager.

"Nah. Can't. Sorry."

If she had hoped for an explanation, none was forthcoming. Instead, Kauri began to wash the breakfast dishes. Stan had already gone into the shop, leaving behind her usual mess.

"I can help you if you like," she offered.

With his back to her, he replied, "I've got it. No worries."

She wanted to ask him if he would be there that evening when she returned, but her pride wouldn't allow it. A final unspoken invitation — leaving the kitchen door open while she went to her room to get her hiking boots — was ignored.

The hike gave Isobel time to organize her thoughts in anticipation of spending the evening alone with her mother. As often happened, she found herself channeling Maggie. The imaginary conversation went back and forth, ending with Maggie telling her to "*stop beating yourself up.*" As she walked down the hill back to her car, Isobel found herself smiling in spite of everything.

~

The woman at the hospital reception desk nodded and smiled at Isobel as she passed. Everyone she had met thus far in New Zealand had been genuinely friendly, and she was beginning to understand why her parents decided to retire here. What would it be like to live here, she wondered? Before her mind could move on to where Vic might fit into this scenario, she arrived at her father's room.

She greeted him with a hug, which he returned with limited strength. This close to him, Isobel noticed his breathing was labored, despite the oxygen tube. Reassuringly, he was not hooked up to any monitors, nor did he have an intravenous line.

"How are you feeling today, Dad?"

"Pretty good. I was looking forward to seeing you, telling you more about Toma."

"You don't have to talk if it's hard for you."

"No. It's important we talk now." The look he gave her carried with it the stark reality of their situation. Time was running out.

"When your mother was here yesterday, she reminded me about something I had forgotten."

He was sitting up straight now, his eyes were alert, his voice filled with energy.

"Remember I told you that you were brought to Canada by a woman from Sarajevo. We used to send her photos of you, hoping she would be able to pass them to Toma and reassure him you were doing fine. When we heard Toma had died, we stopped."

His expression was sad for a moment, but then he brightened.

"After Christina went home last night, she did a Google search and found her, Gordana Leticia. She's still at the university. Christina called me immediately to let me know. I have to admit I'm stunned she remembered the name, and that the woman is still alive after all these years. You should talk with Christina this evening when you go to dinner. Maybe you could contact this Gordana and find out more about your birth mother."

Isobel had not been looking forward to the evening with her mother, negotiating the minefield of their relationship without her father to provide any distraction. This new piece of information changed everything.

They ate in the kitchen as the dining room table had been pushed against one wall of the sitting room to allow space for Novak's wheelchair. Isobel had decided to refrain from saying anything that might provoke a confrontation; she didn't want to alienate her mother in any way this evening. Christina seemed genuinely interested when she asked Isobel about her job at a veterinary clinic and the course work she had to take in order to apply to veterinary school.

"Things were very different when I was growing up on the farm," her mother said. "Vets were few and far between. Sheep either survived or they didn't." She gave a shrug. "Newborn lambs too."

Up to that point Isobel had been enjoying their conversation, but something in her mother's casual indifference to the fate of a newborn lamb prompted a surge of anger she couldn't repress.

"So that's how you saw me. Just another lamb that didn't matter whether it lived or died."

The words came out in a violent explosion of hate. Her mother's head jerked back as if she had slapped her across the face. But Isobel couldn't stop herself. The memory of that evening in Toronto, when her home had been pulled out from under her and the desolation she had felt being left behind, returned with a vengeance.

"You didn't want me. You didn't even try to like me. Never. Not once."

She ripped her napkin from her lap and flung it on the table. Her chair made an ugly scraping noise as she jerked it back.

"Isobel. You've got it wrong. That's not true." Her mother's voice was trembling as she too got up from the table. "Please, please sit down. Hear me out. I can't have you leave like this. Your father would never forgive me."

At the mention of her father, Isobel sat back down reluctantly. Her lips were pressed tightly together, her arms folded.

"Where do I begin?" Christina said, her voice filled with despair.

Her eyes drifted to the wall above Isobel's head as if searching for inspiration.

"When I first met Novak, when we fell in love.... No, you're hardly interested in that." She sighed deeply, the tone of her voice changing and becoming more deliberate. "Novak came home from work one day and told me he'd heard from Toma. I knew he had a brother, but he'd told me they were estranged, so it was a big deal that Toma had reached out to him. Then he told me why — what Toma wanted."

Isobel waited.

"This isn't easy for me either," her mother said, swallowing hard. "Toma wanted us to take you." Again, her mother paused and licked her lips as if it would help the words to come out.

"As Novak mentioned, he and I had agreed right from the beginning that neither of us wanted children. This sudden decision of his seemed a betrayal of sorts. After all, I had a career. I loved my job, and I was good at it. Suddenly, I was going to have to give that up. Even if your father had been willing to be a full-time parent, we couldn't have lived on my nursing salary. He made more than me, but even that was barely enough. We couldn't afford day care. Suddenly *my* world was flipped upside down."

Isobel waited. Her mother's eyes drifted, then returned to engage with Isobel's. She gave the faintest of smiles.

"I loved your father from the first moment I set eyes upon him. I would have done anything for him. So I agreed. After all, you were part of his family, his *whanau*. You know what that means?"

Isobel nodded.

"Sometimes I wonder what would have happened if I had said no. Our marriage wouldn't have survived. But maybe you'd have had a happier childhood. He wouldn't have had to feel so guilty. I *made* him feel guilty. I can see that now. But I resented sharing him with you. I wanted Novak all to myself."

Isobel didn't make any attempt to interrupt the narrative. She owed this to her mother.

"I was never cut out to be a mother." Christina gave a wry chuckle. "But you know that. Still, I was a good nurse, so you never lacked for anything to keep you healthy. You were a colicky baby; I was good at managing that too. It was the only satisfaction I could take from those first months after you arrived. I kept you alive."

This time the silence was longer. Then Isobel noticed a tear making its way down her mother's cheek. Christina wiped it away with her finger.

"There wasn't much love in my home when I was growing up. My parents came from that generation of immigrants who didn't hope for much more than to survive in a new country; they certainly did not expect happiness or fulfillment. My father drank, and my mother just kept her head down and got on with things."

This time Christina didn't bother to wipe away her tears, which welled up quietly and made their way downward to disappear in the collar of her shirt. Isobel found herself at a loss for words. How could she possibly understand what life had been like for Christina? Those first few years in Toronto with Novak would have been the best of her life.

The two women looked at each other across the table, neither sure as to what they had accomplished by baring their souls.

"I'm sorry, Isobel. I wish I could have been a better mother. I did my best."

Isobel gave a long sigh, then smiled at her mother. All of

her anger had dissipated, leaving her feeling profoundly sad for her mother. When she spoke next, her tone was warm.

"Dad was so much better today, and he couldn't wait to tell me about what you found out — about the lady who brought me to Toronto."

Her mother smiled back at her, acknowledging the change.

"Yes. Wasn't that something? When I put the name Gordana Letica into the search box on the university website, a picture of her appeared. I'll get my laptop and show you."

Christina left the room for a few minutes, and Isobel could hear her tapping on the keys of a computer. She returned holding her laptop open.

"There. See. It's the same woman, I'm pretty sure," she said, pointing at the screen. Dr. Gordana Letica had a faculty position in the Institute for Genetics and Biotechnology.

"Is there an email address?" Isobel asked, leaning over her mother's shoulder to look at the image.

Christina scrolled down the page.

"There," Isobel said, pointing to a line of text that read, gordana.letica@unsa.ba. "I'm going to send her an email right now. Do you mind if I use your computer?"

"Of course not. Go right ahead."

Even before her mother answered, Isobel was reaching for the laptop. She began to type rapidly, pausing occasionally to consider how best to phrase her request. She felt as if a lifeline had been extended to her from, quite literally, the grave. Gordana Letica had known her real mother. They had been good friends up until her mother's death. Here was someone who could bring her mother to life inasmuch as that was possible. She needed to meet this woman.

Chapter 22

Isobel had barely crossed the threshold of her father's room at the hospital when he asked, "Have you heard anything yet? Your mother told me you'd sent an email to Gordana." The excitement in his voice was palpable.

Since writing the previous evening, she had checked her inbox regularly. Sarajevo was exactly twelve hours behind New Zealand, which meant her email would have arrived the previous morning. The international date line made things extremely complicated. Her today was Gordana's yesterday. Isobel imagined the woman arriving at her office, opening her computer, and checking her inbox. There was always a possibility the message would be blocked by the university firewall, but Isobel hoped not.

"Nothing so far, Dad. I'll let you know as soon as I hear anything, and if I don't get an email, I'll call her."

A telephone number had been listed in the university directory, but Isobel preferred a written communication. It gave both parties time to gather their thoughts.

Her father was looking even better today. His cheeks had

a little color, and his eyes were alert. He'd had dialysis earlier, a process that took several hours, but at least he didn't have to drive from Motueka. The oxygen tube was gone too, she noticed, and he spoke more easily without needing to take a gulp of air after each sentence. She could see he was wearing his hearing aids, and she moderated her voice accordingly. Pulling out her phone, she checked one more time, then led their conversation back to her father's childhood in Bosnia.

"Our difference in age meant that Toma and I didn't do a lot of things together, but at home he used to follow me around. I suppose he looked up to me. I was good at sports, especially soccer. Our family didn't have the money to go skiing, and it wasn't really a thing in Yugoslavia in those days — not like it is now. Life was pretty simple under Tito, at least for kids, though I'm sure our parents felt differently."

Isobel wanted to ask about her grandparents. Were they alive, and if not, what had happened to them? But she decided not to interrupt. It was more important to find out how her father — her fathers — had become estranged.

"I didn't go to university," Novak continued. "Instead, I got a job at a wood products factory. This was an important industry in Yugoslavia, and getting in on the ground floor in those days meant you had a job for life. In the beginning I couldn't afford to buy a car. Not many people had cars in those days. But eventually I bought a small van. It was a bit of a wreck."

He gave a laugh, but the outburst degenerated into a rough cough that went on for some time. He waited a few minutes before continuing, carefully adjusting his breathing.

"Toma and I spent hours working on that car — the engine, the brakes, the transmission, the rusty undercarriage, everything. I taught him to drive in that van, although he'd probably tell you I wasn't a very good teacher." He gave a half smile as if he could hear his younger brother's voice.

"I did well at the factory — got promoted, a little more money. But there were rumblings about the future, not just in the factory but everywhere. Then Tito died, and all the animosity that had been suppressed while he was in charge surfaced. Toma was at university by that time. The place was a hotbed of Serbian nationalism, and he got sucked in." Shaking his head from side to side, her father gave a grunt of disapproval. "Any time he came home, he'd talk about how Serbs needed to reassert themselves. 'Strong Serbia, Strong Yugoslavia' was the slogan he used to parrot, a phrase Milošević coined. You've heard of him I expect — Milošević? Toma became an ardent supporter."

Novak pressed his lips together, his mouth settling into a hard line.

"By now I could see the writing on the wall. We were heading for a civil war, and it wasn't clear what would happen to my job. After all, I was a Serb working in a Bosnian factory."

In the previous few minutes her father had become agitated, and Isobel noticed he was rubbing the edge of the bedspread between his fingers and thumb as if trying to brush something off. She interrupted him, asking if he needed a glass of water, but he shook his head. He was becoming visibly tired now.

"I left Yugoslavia in 1990. Our mother had died years earlier. She died of breast cancer when Toma was thirteen. Dad said he was too old to leave, although I tried to persuade him to come with me. He came from a generation that had never learned to speak a foreign language and knew he'd be lost in Canada. By the time I left, Toma and I were no longer speaking to each other. We had nothing in common anymore."

Her father stopped talking abruptly, closed his eyes, and sank back into the pillows. Isobel put her hand on his, if only to reassure herself that he was still alive.

"Thanks for telling me this, Dad. I know it's painful for you, but it means everything to me."

She glanced at her phone, which she had placed face up on the bedside stand.

"Nothing from Gordana yet," she said.

Her father's eyelids flickered.

"It's only five a.m. there. Maybe I'll hear something later this evening. If not, I'll try calling her tomorrow."

Kauri wasn't at Stan's Place when she got back from the hospital. Neither was Stan. The book Kauri had been reading was sitting on her bedside table. She grabbed it and riffled through the pages. Nothing. She sat on the bed, idly smoothing the bedclothes, then buried her head in them and inhaled deeply. Kauri's smell lingered. Strangely, she found that she didn't harbor any resentment towards him, nor did she feel she had been abandoned.

There was a note from Stan on the kitchen table. "Got an unexpected client. Back in a couple of days." With Stan, a couple of days could mean anything, so Isobel walked around to the front of the shop. A piece of paper with identical words was taped to the window beside the closed sign, confirming that both Stan and her nephew were gone. Mentally adjusting to this new situation, Isobel walked across the street to the Beached Whale and ordered a basket of fish and chips and a glass of wine.

Returning to the empty house an hour later, she opened

her computer and checked her email. There was a message from Gordana. Her heart rate quickened as she fumbled to open it. The tone of the letter was stilted, as if it had been written first in another language and then translated into English using Google Translate. She scanned the letter, searching for any indication that Gordana might be willing to meet with her. The second time she read it more slowly, trying to get a sense of how the woman might want to relate to her after all these years. It reminded Isobel of when she had first made contact with Lara, Maggie's daughter. She had written to Lara asking if she would want to meet her birth mother after fifty years. To Isobel it had been the culmination of months of sleuthing and a satisfying conclusion to the project she had embarked upon without Maggie's knowledge. At the time she felt confident Maggie would want to know what sort of person her daughter had become. But this situation was different. This time Isobel's own birth mother, Amela, was the subject of her search, or rather, the ghost of her birth mother.

While Gordana's email didn't exactly invite Isobel to Sarajevo, the woman said she would be in the city for the remainder of the semester as she was teaching a class at the university. With fingers flying across the keyboard, Isobel responded that she would come to Sarajevo just as soon as she could organize a flight.

CHAPTER 23

To her dismay, Isobel discovered it would take almost three days to get from Kaiteriteri to Sarajevo. She would arrive early on a Friday morning, and while she would have liked to meet Gordana that same day, she knew it would take her some time to recover from the trip, as well as adjust to the twelve-hour time difference. She wanted to be fully alert for their meeting.

She left New Zealand the following morning, feeling the effects of too little sleep but buoyed by the prospect of finally going home. She'd written a long email to Vic, telling him about Toma and about contacting Gordana and her plan to stop in Sarajevo before returning to the United States. She'd ended the letter with "Can't wait to see you!" hoping the absence of "I love you" would not be noticed. One part of her was certain she loved him. However, the fact that she was typing the email sitting in a bed that smelled of lovemaking with another man was not lost on her.

With a last look around Stan's Place, she climbed into her car and headed south along the Ruby Coast for the last time. Her only regret was that she couldn't say goodbye to Stan in person. Rarely had she felt such kinship with another woman in such a short time. Stan was a force of nature and someone she wished could be in her life forever. Isobel had spent a considerable time composing the letter she left propped up on the kitchen counter. In it were details of her plans — drive to Nelson to return the rental car, then fly to Christchurch, New Zealand, Singapore, Frankfurt, and finally Sarajevo. The remainder of the letter contained a sincere thank you to Stan for being a steady guide not just on the trail but also in how to cope during this tumultuous time. She had hesitated before asking Stan to share the news with Kauri. After all, she would never see him again so what did it matter? But still, he was part of Stan's *whanau*, and Isobel felt she owed him that much. Then, uncertain as to how to pay for her stay, she left three hundred dollars on the table and, as a final gesture, stripped her bed of its soiled sheets and put them in the washing machine. At the last minute, she picked up the book Kauri had been reading and slipped it into her backpack.

On the way to Nelson, Isobel planned to stop first at her mother's house and then at the hospital. She had called her mother the previous evening, although it was quite late, to tell her that Gordana had responded and that she was flying to Sarajevo. For the first time, she felt that her mother was genuinely happy for her. They had arrived at a rapprochement of sorts, no longer needing to compete, both recognizing they needed to share whatever time Novak had left. She dreaded saying goodbye to both of them.

Even before she had a chance to press the buzzer, the door opened. Her mother's face was a tight mask of suppressed emotion.

"I'm not going to cry. If I start now, I'll never stop," she said.

Isobel could see the muscles of her cheeks contract as she swallowed hard.

"I don't think I can be that brave," Isobel replied, tears welling up in her eyes.

Her mother pulled her into a tight hug. It was such an unfamiliar gesture to Isobel that she tensed initially, before relaxing and allowing herself to be comforted. She wept on her mother's shoulder, great heaving sobs that contained years of pent-up yearning for love. Her mother gently disengaged, then held Isobel by her shoulders and looked directly into her eyes.

"I am so glad you came to us. It has made Novak so very happy."

Isobel waited, knowing her mother was struggling to find the right words.

"You and I have had our differences in the past. I hope the future will be better."

Isobel knew her mother had crossed a chasm of sorts. They went into the house, her mother holding Isobel's arm as if she was afraid that when she let it go, she would be letting go of Novak too.

"You know that picture you have in the sitting room, Mom, the one from my high school graduation? If it's okay, I'd like to take a photo of it."

"Of course you can. I'd give you the picture, but your father is very fond of it. We both are."

Isobel moved the picture frame slightly so light would not reflect off the glass. She pointed to the blemished wood underneath.

"I remember that stain, Mom. It was my fault. But the picture does a great job of hiding it." She laughed and was pleased to see her mother laughing too.

"I'll have a proper copy made and send it to you," her mother said.

They talked for a little while, but neither of them wanted to prolong this farewell. Their final hug was brief but carried with it the sincerity of a new understanding. The pain she felt on saying goodbye to her mother surprised Isobel. All the hate and resentment she had nurtured for years had evaporated, replaced by something approaching love. Leaving the house for the last time, she braced herself for the next farewell with its utter finality.

Isobel's mouth was dry when she walked into the hospital, and she barely acknowledged the greeting from the familiar receptionist. She took the stairs to the third floor, steeling herself, delaying the moment when she would see her father.

He was waiting for her, the door to his room wide open. When she walked in, he smiled immediately, stretching his arms out to greet her. She glanced at the other bed in the room, hoping that it was still unoccupied. She didn't want anyone to witness her anguish.

"Hi Dad. You're looking better today." Her voice was unnaturally cheerful.

"I'm feeling pretty good. I think they might let me go home tomorrow."

Isobel pulled a chair over to the side of the bed.

"Mom told you about Gordana?"

He nodded. "She called me this morning early to tell me." His eyes lit up and he gave a little chuckle. "So, you're going to Sarajevo? Going back to where you were born?"

"Yes. I'm excited, although it's going to take almost three days to get there."

"Does Gordana know you're coming?"

"Yeah. I sent her an email once I had my flights arranged.

I'll get there on Friday, but I won't be meeting with her until Monday."

She steeled herself, remembering what her mother said about not crying. Isobel knew that if she started now, she too would not be able to stop. She didn't want to make this parting any harder.

"I wish we had more time together," her father said.

Isobel took his hand in hers, feeling the combination of warmth and frailty. Her other hand she kept in her lap, alternately digging her nails into her palm, then releasing them. The pain helped her maintain some level of composure.

"I'm so glad I came to New Zealand, Dad." Even though she spoke the truth, the statement sounded banal, and she quickly added, "It's meant everything to me. Not just learning about who I am but understanding what you and Mom did. I had no idea. You were...you *are* amazing parents, and I am incredibly lucky to have you in my life. I know you're my uncle, but you'll always be my dad."

Her father squeezed her hand. Nothing could prevent the tears that were welling up in her eyes.

"You should get going. You've got a long journey ahead of you."

She hesitated.

"Go. Go."

With a final squeeze, her father let go of her hand. She stood up and leaned in to give him a final kiss before tearing herself away. Blinded by tears, she gripped the handrail as she made her way down the stairs and out to the car.

∼

The evening flight from Nelson to Christchurch took

barely an hour. That was followed by a midnight departure to Singapore. Isobel managed to catch up on sleep during the eleven-hour flight. She began reading Kauri's book on the flight to Frankfurt, another thirteen hours in the air. He had been right about *The Bone People*. It was a thoroughly absorbing read, all the more so because of its underlying theme — a search for family.

When she finally arrived in Sarajevo, she was beyond exhaustion and immediately took a taxi to her hotel. Waking later that afternoon in yet another unfamiliar bed, Isobel stared up at the ceiling, allowing her thoughts to wander. She was surprised when her phone rang, and even more when the caller's name appeared: Vic. She had sent him her itinerary, so he knew she would be in Sarajevo by now. Only seven hours separated them, or was it eight? Whichever, it was a Friday morning in Wisconsin.

"I thought you might try to call me here. It's great to hear your voice," she said, reassured that her voice held no trace of insincerity.

"It's so good to finally be able to talk to you," he said with a relieved sigh, the sound of which was amplified by the echo in the connection. "I've missed you so much. Oliver has missed you so much. I wish he could talk because then he and I could sympathize with each other." He laughed at his own whimsy. "How are you? Tell me everything."

Shocked to realize it had been ten days since she last spoke with Vic, she proceeded to give him a rundown of what had happened.

"We could talk face-to-face if you like," Isobel said eventually, "although I don't remember if your computer is set up for that. We've never had to do it before."

"There's no need, and anyway, you'll be home in a few

days. Besides, I still remember what you look like." He gave a chuckle.

"Yeah. Wednesday evening. I'll be looking for you."

"I'll be there."

She waited for him to say something more.

"So, have you met with Gordana yet?" He pronounced the name with an emphasis on the second syllable, whereas her father had put the stress on the first.

"No. That's not until Monday. I thought I might be able to meet with her tomorrow, but she's busy over the weekend. Instead, I'm going to take in the sights of Sarajevo, that is if I don't fall asleep. It was an exhausting trip — something like fifty-five hours." She gave a little laugh. "I didn't think it was possible to spend that much time in airports and planes. I feel sorry for business travelers. There were lots of them on the flights with me, all looking dazed and shell-shocked."

Once she said the word out loud, Isobel realized how inappropriate the metaphor was and made a mental note to be more circumspect when she spoke with Gordana, or anyone else who had lived through the Bosnian war. She chatted for a little longer with Vic, voicing her nervousness about the upcoming conversation with Gordana. Granted the woman had delivered her to Toronto, but then she had disappeared from Isobel's life. What sort of a friend had she been to Amela after all? Vic tried to reassure her, pointing out that there was a war going on at the time and perhaps Gordana had her own problems. Isobel was somewhat mollified by this explanation, and their conversation ended on a more upbeat note.

On Saturday morning she joined a guided bus tour of the main war sites in the city. The English-speaking guide, a pleasant-looking woman in her fifties, described herself as a

Sarajevan first and foremost but added for clarification that she had been raised as a Croatian Catholic. She emphasized how well everyone got along in Sarajevo before the war — Serbs, Croats, and Bosnians — and how quickly everything changed. The guide had lived in the city during the forty-four-month siege, losing many friends and family members. As she enumerated the dates of the siege, beginning in April 1992, Isobel realized that if her adoption papers were correct, she had been born in the midst of that carnage. She followed the guide in a daze, hardly absorbing anything more the woman said. Almost every building was pockmarked with bullet holes. The tour bus drove through Sniper Alley, an area in the center of the city where snipers were positioned in tower blocks during the war, shooting at anything that moved. Isobel could only think of one thing. What must it have been like for her mother, pregnant and trapped?

The bus took them to the site of the 1984 Olympic Winter Games. Standing in the Olympic Village, the city lying beneath her in a panorama, it was easy to see why this had been the location of choice for the Serbian artillery to shell the city. The final stop on the tour was a recently erected monument to children killed during the siege. Seven pedestals beside the glass monument had the names of five hundred children etched into them, although the guide told them the number of children killed was far greater than this — sixteen hundred at least. It came as a shock to Isobel to realize that the names of all those other children were lost, that nobody could document their existence. Had their entire families been killed too?

The following afternoon, as she sat at a café in the Old Town area of Sarajevo, the horrors of the previous day were replaced by a modern, cosmopolitan scene. Around her she could hear German, Italian, and Spanish being spoken in addition to the guttural vowels of Bosnian, Serbian, and Croatian. These unfamiliar local languages were indistinguishable to Isobel, giving her renewed respect for the professor of Slavic studies, who she had asked for help.

A young woman with a crown on her head and holding a bouquet of flowers, laughed as she skipped up the steps of a fountain in the town square, her hen party entourage trailing behind her. Isobel tried to eavesdrop, curious as to where they were from, but the plaza was too noisy. Were any of these people looking for personal traces of the war, she wondered? Was anyone else looking to find the ghosts of their parents? The word parent had taken on a new meaning for her over the past weeks. Prior to leaving the United States, she saw her adoptive parents as remote, both physically and emotionally. Now she looked upon them in a very different light. Her biological parents had also come into a clearer focus. Two young people had fallen in love here, in this city, and had a child together. Although dead for many years, tomorrow she would get the opportunity to make them as real as possible.

Chapter 24

Isobel walked past the park where she had seen the children's monument, past the American Embassy and a statue of Tito, to a tree-lined alley off the main thoroughfare that led to Gordana's building, the Institute of Genetic Engineering and Biotechnology. It wasn't a pretty campus. Her first impression was of hastily constructed, functional buildings with none of the grandeur one might expect from an institution that boasted its origins in the 1500s. In reality, the university had opened its doors after the Second World War. Most of its buildings had come under fire during the Bosnian war, and even now the damage was apparent, with blemished walls and paths.

She found the building, a single-story concrete structure with barred windows. A small plaque beside the entrance to the building showed a red and blue DNA symbol with the letters INGEB to the left of it. Passing through two sets of doors, she stepped into a long narrow corridor lined with offices. The sign for Forensic Genetics was easy to recognize, as the Bosnian words were similar to English — Laboratorija za Forenzičku Genetiku. The first door on the left had a nameplate with "Dr.

Gordana Letica" on it and something else written under the name that Isobel assumed must mean "head of laboratory," for that was her official title. Isobel checked her phone; she was a little early. She paused to calm herself before knocking.

An accented voice said in English, "Please come in."

Gordana Letica stood when Isobel entered the small, spartan office. Based on her career, Isobel had calculated she must be in her early 60s. She wore no makeup and looked pale in the harsh fluorescent light that reflected off her black sweater.

"Hello," Isobel said, her voice sounding slightly shaky. She could see the woman scrutinizing her face.

"I didn't expect you to look so much like her," Gordana said. "It's almost as if Amela walked out of our building that morning and has just now come back."

Isobel noticed the woman's hands were gripped tightly in front of her as if she was making an effort to keep her composure.

"I'm sorry. I just need a moment...." Gordana swallowed hard. "I have forgotten my manners. Please sit down."

She gestured to a chair facing a plain metal desk. The two women faced each other, neither quite sure how to begin their conversation. Finally, Gordana broke the silence.

"I'm so glad you found me. I have spent years wondering what happened to you. And then, suddenly, out of nowhere, you appear. I cannot believe it. How did you find me?"

It took Isobel some time to answer the question, abbreviating her life story as much as possible. Occasionally, Gordana interrupted her, especially when she spoke too quickly or used jargon. Some minutes later and with the outline of the story delivered, Isobel sat back with a sigh. Then both women began to speak at the same time.

"Forgive me. Please go ahead," Gordana said, making a gesture with her hands. "You must have many questions."

Isobel nodded, acknowledging the invitation.

"But you must have known about those first few years in Canada. Dad told me he wrote to you in the beginning and sent you photos of me. He thought you might be able to give them to Toma."

"No, that was not possible." Gordana shook her head emphatically. "If he wrote to me here at the university, those letters would not have been delivered. Not during the war. And I was not here. I did not return to Sarajevo after I took you to Canada."

Gordana's eyes were suddenly alert.

"Do you realize that taking you to Canada probably saved my life? If I had returned to Sarajevo, I might have been killed. So many people were. Ordinary people, just going about their lives."

They sat in silence for a while, each of them contemplating how capricious life could be. Isobel scanned Gordana's face, trying to interpret the woman's changing expressions. Regret, sadness, resignation, anger — they were all present.

"The war started on a Sunday," Gordana began, the corners of her mouth sinking into the lines etched there. "I remember because my brother was coming back from the sports center at Skenderija on the trolley, and he said it was held up by a bunch of men wearing balaclavas and carrying Kalashnikovs. Someone had been shot by a Serb at a rally in the center of the city, a rally to keep Sarajevo out of a war we all knew was coming." She sighed.

"Our lives were being poisoned by a man called Radovan Karadžić, who claimed that it was impossible for people of different nationalities to live together in Bosnia. This was a lie. Muslims and Serbs and Croats had lived together here for hundreds of years. We went to the same schools, played with each other, fell in love and married each other. Maybe the old people didn't approve of intermarriage. But for us — for my generation — it was normal."

Isobel hung on every word.

"Your mother and I knew each other from the university. She was doing a project in molecular biology and spent a lot of time in my laboratory. We got to know each other well. I was a little bit older than her, but not by much. We used to party together. Sarajevo had a great nighttime scene before the war."

She smiled then, and for a brief moment Isobel could visualize her mother and Gordana as young women enjoying their life at university.

"Things changed quickly after that. Serb shelling was destroying the city, demolishing many apartment buildings, including the one where I was living. Your mother said I could move in with her. She had an apartment on an upper floor, but eventually that became too dangerous. Everyone in her building moved to the basement. It was very crowded, but at least it was safe from the bombs.

"That first year of the siege was so cold. There was no fuel, no electricity. We burned anything we could find to stay warm. Sometimes I look around and try to remember what it was like here at the university in those days. Imagine, we burned most of the furniture. And yet we kept on trying to do our work, our research and teaching."

Gordana clasped the edge of the desk with her fingers. Isobel could see that she was struggling with what she was about to say.

"When your mother was killed, I did not know what to do. You were four months old."

Gordana looked out through the small, barred window, then turned back to face Isobel.

"Amela left you with me that day. She was hoping to barter some things for food at the market. It was a risk, of course, but we had very little money left." She gave a little shrug. "There were always snipers. You just got used to it. People would tell you which streets to avoid. The mortar attacks came at any time. There was nothing you could do except hope you were lucky that day.

"When Amela didn't return that evening, I knew something was wrong. I remember you were crying. She was still breast-feeding you, and you were hungry. Another mother there fed you. She had a baby a little younger than you. Everybody helped everyone else — it was the only way to survive. The next day we heard what had happened. It was a mortar shell. It killed your mother and many others at the market."

They sat in silence, the only sound a hum from the ceiling light fixture. Isobel desperately wanted to run out of the claustrophobic room and get as far away as possible from this damaged city. Instead, she forced herself to sit and listen to every piece of information Gordana was willing to recollect.

"I found your father's telephone number in Amela's satchel. The telephones were still working here at the university. I told him what had happened and asked when he was going to come and get you. I don't remember exactly what he said, something like, 'I need to make arrangements.' Three weeks later I got a message from him saying that if I was willing to take you to his brother in Toronto, I could leave the city safely. He would make sure of it."

She stood up abruptly and paced behind her desk. Isobel didn't dare speak or move a muscle, afraid she might interrupt the narrative. Gordana sat down again and continued.

"After I delivered you to Novak, I made the decision not to come back to Sarajevo. One part of me felt like a traitor for abandoning the city, but I couldn't continue with my work. Our research labs were destroyed, and most of the equipment had been looted. The university could not pay our salaries. It took years before things began to return to normal.

"I had friends in Italy at the University of Padua who offered me a temporary position. I went there directly from Canada and stayed for the next five years. It felt wrong to not be in Sarajevo. You know, Padua is only eight hundred kilometers from here. I thought about coming back many times, but by then all the roads were sealed off. I suppose I might have been able to get in through the tunnel — there was an underground tunnel from the airport into the city — try to find my colleagues, bring some things from Italy. But they didn't need scientific equipment or reagents. They needed food and medicine. They needed the war to end."

Gordana looked directly at Isobel, her eyebrows raised. "Perhaps I was a coward?"

Isobel declined to answer, choosing instead to bring the narrative back to her parents.

"Did you know my father?"

"I met him a couple of times."

She leaned forward, as if her gesture could urge Gordana to tell her more.

"I think they started to see each other sometime around 1988 or 1989. I suppose they met at university, though I'm not sure. By the time I got to know your mother, Toma had become a shadowy figure. She did not talk much about him. But she would get that look in her eye when she said she had to leave the lab early or if she arrived to work later in the morning. It was not a regular thing. I think he must have left the university by then because she mentioned once that her boyfriend lived in Banja Luca. That city was a Serbian stronghold during the war."

"Tell me more about my mother, about Amela." Isobel's voice was urgent now.

Saying her mother's name aloud felt strange. Isobel wanted to roll the word around in her mouth and lick her lips as if she could taste the essence of her mother, smell her, feel her warmth. The image of a woman huddled in a basement and breastfeeding a child came to mind, and she began to tear up.

Gordana smiled at her acquiescence. She took some time to describe her friend, recalling every detail she could remember of the young, happy student who had recently given birth to a baby girl. She had no photographs — they were lost in the war — so Isobel conjured up a girl much like herself at twenty-three, embellishing the picture with the details Gordana provided. The color of her eyes, the length and color of her mother's hair, her height, the freckles on her face and arms.

Brushing the tears from her cheeks, Isobel asked, "Where is she buried?"

She could see the pain in Gordana's eyes. She waited, holding her breath.

"I do not know where she is buried. There were so many bodies. They say fourteen thousand people were killed in the city. You would pass dead bodies lying in the street, sometimes just parts of bodies.... They might be there for days."

She looked away, her eyes unfocused as if she could rid herself of some of those images.

"Most people have come to accept that anyone not accounted for is buried in the cemetery on the hillside overlooking the city. That is where they go to mourn."

Gordana glanced at her watch. "I'm sorry but I have to go. I have to give a lecture in a few minutes."

They had talked for only two hours, yet Isobel felt she had lived through two full lifetimes.

"Perhaps we could meet again before I go back to the States? I'm leaving the day after tomorrow. Would you have any time free between now and then?"

Gordana opened her laptop to check her calendar.

"Tomorrow, later in the day, say three p.m.?" She paused for a moment, then asked, "But won't you go to Verona before you go back to the United States?"

Isobel was puzzled. "Verona?"

"Yes, Verona. To see Toma — your father."

Chapter 25

Not trusting her legs to carry her safely to the street, Isobel clung to the railing as she went down the steps from the building. Toma was alive. A single question bounced around in her brain like a noisy pinball, drowning out everything else. Why had he not tried to find her? After all, he knew where she lived. Maybe he didn't care? But he *had* cared. He had made sure she was safe, far from Sarajevo and with someone who would take care of her. Oblivious to her surroundings on the walk back to her hotel, her mind fixated on a single fact — her real father was living in Verona.

Her first thought as soon as she got to her room was that she should email Novak and tell him his brother was still alive. She opened her computer and began to type, then stopped abruptly as a flurry of questions raced through her mind. Should she be the one to tell him? It might lift his spirits, especially now. But why hadn't Toma reached out to Novak before this? Maybe he hadn't wanted to, in which case it would be cruel to tell her father about his brother. Isobel felt torn, but in the end decided that she needed to meet Toma before doing anything.

She typed in the query, How to get from Sarajevo to Verona? A map appeared, a heavy blue line coursing up and left on the screen, passing through Croatia and Slovenia into the north of Italy. She noted the line went through Venice, a city she had always wanted to visit. The distance was nine hundred kilometers and according to the web page, would take nine and a half hours to drive. A road trip of that distance would be easy in the United States, but here it was far more complicated. She would have to arrange a one-way car rental, if that was even possible, considering she would be traveling through several countries. Otherwise, she would have to return the car in Sarajevo. The drive wouldn't be easy either, with road signs in unfamiliar languages, none of which she understood. Moving to the next option, she searched for flights. Several airlines popped up on her screen, but none offered direct flights. Every plane was routed through Germany and took almost as much time as driving. Another query, this time for trains, but there were no trains between the two cities. Wasn't Europe famous for its train service? She tapped her fingers with irritation at the edge of her keyboard, then tried another search. There had to be a bus? After all, not everyone in Europe owned a car. Another thick line appeared on the screen, this time in black. It would be a sixteen-hour trip with at least two changes, but at least there would be something to look at along the way, she reasoned. Moreover, she could get off the bus at any time, in Venice for example, and resume the journey later.

She had a plan.

∼

The following afternoon, when Isobel knocked on Gordana's office door, every one of her nerve endings was tingling with excitement. The previous night she had hardly slept, and the morning had dragged, despite her taking a long walk through the city to try to distract herself. Gordana greeted her warmly and apologized for leaving so abruptly the previous day, explaining that her lectures were attended by over a hundred students, whose classes were tightly scheduled.

"I thought you might prefer to talk over a coffee," Gordana said, getting up from her desk and slipping her laptop into her satchel. "My lectures are finished for today. There is a place not far from here that is quiet. We can take my car."

"Coffee would be great," Isobel said, trying to hide her eagerness. She would have preferred to have her questions answered immediately but recognized that Gordana might need a little time to gather her thoughts after giving a lecture.

As they left the building, Isobel remarked, "There are bars on the windows. Is that necessary?"

"Ah yes. The bars. I'm afraid so. This is the biggest forensic genetics laboratory in Bosnia-Herzegovina. We do DNA analysis here for police and for paternity testing. But our other major focus is identifying the remains of the dead." She stopped briefly and turned to face Isobel. "Even though the war has been over for more than twenty years, there are deep scars, and many people do not want the truth to come out."

They drove to a quiet neighborhood and found a parking spot near the café. Trees shaded several outdoor tables, but it was chilly, and the tables were empty. Inside, the space was decorated in a modern Euro style with a tile floor and shiny surfaces, unlike the café where Isobel had been two days earlier. There she had sipped thick Turkish coffee served in a copper pot and watched as a group seated nearby on velvet cushions shared a hookah. While they waited for the barista to deliver their order, Isobel made small talk, commenting on the merits of cappuccino versus a flat white, which she admitted growing fond of in New Zealand. Their coffees delivered, Isobel took a sip, then sat back in her chair and waited for Gordana. There was no need for her to prompt. They both knew the importance of this conversation.

"Toma contacted me six years ago. Until then I had assumed that, if he survived the war, he would be living somewhere in Republika Srbska. People like him were heroes there, not the undesirables they would be if they came back to Sarajevo. No matter what they did in the war, they would be safe in Srbska." The look of disgust on Gordana's face was unmistakable. "A letter came with an Italian postmark. I thought it must be from one of my colleagues in Padua, but when I opened it, I saw it was written in Serbian. It was signed, Toma Babić."

She paused to take a sip of her coffee.

"Toma explained he was living in Verona under a different name — Paolo Parma." She said the name with an Italian accent. "He wanted to know if I knew how to contact Novak. He had written to Novak's address in Toronto, but the letter was returned to him unopened." She frowned. "I was very surprised. After all, it had been twenty years. There was no telephone number with Toma's letter, so I wrote back saying I had not heard from Novak since I brought you to Canada. I explained that I did not come back to Sarajevo but went to Padua instead." She shook her head. "Toma did not reply. I have heard nothing from him since."

Isobel barely noticed that her coffee had grown cold.

"Did you keep the letter? Do you still have his address in Verona?" The words tumbled out of her mouth.

"Yes and yes." Gordana bent down to retrieve her satchel, took out an envelope, and handed it to Isobel.

"May I?" Isobel was already opening the flap.

"Of course. But you will not be able to understand anything, I think. The name and the address are easy to read though — Paolo Parma, Apartment 3B, 12 Via Francesco Berni, Verona. I remember looking up where it was at the time. It's near the train station. Are you going to go there?"

"I think so. I have to, don't I?"

"You could write to him."

"But I'm here now, and it's only five hundred miles away."

Gordana's tone was gentle when she asked the question. "What if he doesn't want to meet you?"

Isobel gave a sigh. "I've thought about that. Lots of men don't want to meet their children, especially if they've abandoned them. But he didn't really abandon me, did he? He made sure I was all right after..."

She clamped her lips tightly together, not wanting to reiterate the horror of the past.

The espresso machine hissed in the background as they sat in silence, each of them unsure as to what to say next. Then Gordana's face softened into an expression of genuine tenderness as she looked at Isobel.

"You were one of the lucky ones. Whatever happens in Verona, remember that."

The conversation was over. There would be other questions, Isobel was certain, but for now they had both said enough. As if she read Isobel's mind, Gordana opened her satchel and took out a card with her home address and cell phone number.

"You can contact me at any time," she said passing the card to Isobel, "and perhaps you will tell me what you find in Verona."

"Can I ask you one last question?"

"Of course."

"I know my father was Serbian and my mother was Bosnian. Are you Bosnian too?"

Gordana considered the question carefully before answering.

"You know, young people today don't seem to care so much about these names. Me? I am a European."

She got up from her chair, came around to Isobel, and kissed her on both cheeks.

"Amela would be very proud of you."

Chapter 26

The pain in her right side began somewhere north of Zagreb. Isobel thought it might be a cramp at first. She had been sitting for several hours by then, and despite the bus stopping every two hours for passengers to stretch their legs, this ten-hour segment of the journey seemed interminable. At the bus station in Ljubljana, where she was to board a Slovenian coach bound for Venice, she used the three-hour layover to get something to eat. Within half an hour of finishing her meal, she rushed to the bathroom and threw up. The pain in her side persisted, despite taking two Tylenol. The next bus was barely half full, and she chose a window seat at the back, close to the bathroom. An hour or so later. to distract herself, she went to get Kauri's book from her pack only to discover she had left it behind at the bus station in Ljubljana. By the time she arrived in Venice three hours later, she had jettisoned any thought of taking a tour of the city.

The bus finally pulled into Verona. By now she was beginning to worry. Tylenol had done nothing for the pain, which was all-consuming. She sat on a bench outside the bus station, her suitcase and pack at her feet, taking deep breaths in the hope that it might help. The wail of an ambulance in the distance was a blunt reminder that she had no options. She knew no one in the city, and even if her father was still living here, she didn't have his telephone number. Dragging herself to her feet, she struggled to the taxi stand and knocked on the window of the solitary vehicle parked there.

"*Dove?*" he asked when he had rolled down the window.

"Hospital," Isobel said, enunciating the word.

"*Ospedale?*" His eyebrows were raised. Then he said something she didn't understand.

"Emergency," she replied, clutching at her stomach.

She must have looked ill, for he got out of the car to help her into the back seat, then put her suitcase and backpack in the trunk. Five minutes later they drove up to a covered entrance where an ambulance was parked. While the taxi driver unloaded her luggage, a woman with a clipboard came over to Isobel and said something.

"English? Do you speak any English?" Isobel asked in a strained voice.

"A little. What is wrong?"

Pointing to her lower right side, Isobel said, "I have a pain, here." She had straightened to show the location and for a moment thought she might faint.

"Come," the woman said, gesturing towards the entrance hall.

Isobel was about to lift her backpack, but the woman took it from her.

"Come," she said again, extending the handle of Isobel's bag and wheeling it into the building.

There were several other people seated in the waiting area. The woman pointed Isobel to a chair in front of a desk on which there was a computer and gestured that she should sit down. She left, and soon afterwards a new person appeared and slid into the empty chair facing Isobel.

To her relief, she heard the woman say, "I speak some English."

After taking her name, date of birth, and nationality, the medical questions were brief. Where exactly was the pain? For how long had she had it? Did she have a fever? Were there any other symptoms? Had she been sick recently? The woman explained that the hospital used a triage system, with ambulance cases or those who were very sick seen first. She motioned Isobel to a row of benches and said she would be called in a while.

Isobel pulled her credit card out of her purse and offered it to the woman.

"There is no need for that," the woman said, shaking her head. "This is a public hospital. There is no charge."

Time passed slowly while the pain gnawed at her. The benches were made of hard plastic, and she could find no comfortable position. Had someone asked her at that moment what she wanted most in the world, she would have said, "To go home." If she were at home, she could have driven herself to the emergency room at the hospital in Sauk City, barely ten minutes from the house, confident that whatever was wrong could be fixed. Vic would arrive soon after, his face a mask of concern. In his steady way, he would reassure her that everything was going to be all right. She closed her eyes, as if doing so might diminish her panic.

Half an hour later someone touched her elbow, and she gave a start. This nurse said her name and nodded when Isobel repeated it. She gestured for Isobel to follow. Dragging her bag and backpack, she went through a set of double doors into a large ward where a dozen or more people were lying on beds. It was so different from any emergency room she had been to in the United States, where privacy demanded that everything take place behind a screen or a closed door. The nurse motioned for her to sit on a bed and roll up her sleeve. Isobel watched numbly as three vials of blood were drawn. Next, she was directed to another bank of chairs where she sat and waited. Meanwhile, the bed where she had been was quickly occupied by another patient.

With nothing to do, she opened her cell phone and was dismayed to see she only had five percent of battery life left. She used the remaining minutes to find out exactly where she was. According to the little blue dot on the screen, the taxi driver had brought her to the Borgo Trento hospital, which, according to its web page, was a teaching hospital in the northern suburbs of the city. She thought about trying to contact Vic but decided against it. Her cell phone would probably die in the middle of the call. And besides, if she said that she was sitting in an emergency room at a hospital in Verona, what could he possibly do?

To take her mind off the pain, she went over the last conversation she had with him a couple of days earlier. She heard the irritation in his voice the moment he answered. It was understandable. She had caught him at one of his work sites — a house addition for a demanding client who changed his mind at every turn, then blamed Vic for the cost overruns.

"I'm sorry, Isobel, but I can't talk right now. We'll be seeing each other in a couple of days. Can it wait until then?"

"No, it can't. Can you give me just a few minutes?"

"Okay. Let me tell my client that I need to take this call."

He came back a couple of minutes later. That's when she

broke the news to him that her biological father was alive, and that she had decided to go to Verona to see him. The silence that followed brought a chill of cold Wisconsin air. Isobel tried to explain but found herself up against a wall of resentment. Then abruptly Vic changed the subject.

"I got another letter from the lawyer in Massachusetts, the one representing Lara. She's accusing me of being involved in Maggie's death, of not getting Maggie to a hospital quickly enough or something like that." His voice cracked. "But she was already dead when we found her. There was nothing I could do."

"What exactly did the letter say?" Isobel asked cautiously.

"The lawyer is requesting the police report, the toxicology report, all that stuff."

"Did he ask for her medical records? It should be clear from them she had terminal cancer. And there was her suicide note. What happened to that?"

"I gave it to my lawyer. Good thing I kept it. Say, do you still have the letter she wrote to you from Ireland? Didn't she say that she was going to kill herself there but changed her mind when she heard you had found Lara? Together they should be enough to show her intentions."

Isobel tried to sound positive. "I'll check as soon as I get home."

Vic didn't state the obvious, that she was delaying her homecoming by going to Verona.

"I'm beyond worry, Isobel. I mean I'm working as hard as I can, and every day it seems there's something else. It's killing me. Please, please come home soon."

She vacillated between guilt and anger. He should have been excited for her, should have reassured her that going to Verona was absolutely the right thing to do. Instead, he was being selfish and unreasonable. She was afraid of saying something she would regret.

"Do you want me to transfer some money to you right now?"

It came out sounding sharp, so she added quickly, "The last time we talked, you said you might need some money to pay the lawyer."

The irony of the situation did not escape Isobel. Maggie would be paying for the validation of her own suicide.

"That would help a lot. You know I'll pay you back. It's just a cash flow thing right now."

She could hear muffled words in the background, and Vic's voice directed at someone else. He came back on the line.

"I'm sorry Isobel but I have to go. The guy is getting impatient."

"Why don't you email me your account number and the routing code. I'll transfer ten thousand."

They had ended the call with perfunctory I love you's, which hadn't satisfied or reassured Isobel. She wondered if Vic had felt the same.

A man came over to where Isobel was sitting. In Italian, mixed with fragmented English, he explained that she was to follow him to have an ultrasound. He led her to a small examination room where two women, both wearing white coats, were waiting for her. From her days working in the veterinary clinic, Isobel knew that this procedure should not be painful. Nonetheless, she tensed when one of the women smeared gel over her abdomen and began to move the ultrasound probe around. The women spoke rapidly to each other throughout the procedure, but Isobel couldn't catch even the gist of what they were saying. When her abdomen was wiped clean of gel, she was motioned to dress and then pointed in the direction of the large ward where she had waited previously.

Sitting by her luggage, nobody took any notice of her, and she was uncertain what would happen next. Around her people waited patiently, some seated, others lying on gurneys or hospital beds. She crossed the ward to the water dispenser but was intercepted by the same man as before. He made a gesture with his finger, wagging it from side to side, and shook his head.

"No food. No water."

She returned to her seat and tried to suppress her growing alarm. The pain was intensifying. Soon afterwards, a nurse came for her and led her to another room where a man wearing a white coat was waiting. A doctor, she thought, judging by the degree of respect the nurse had shown. To her intense relief, he spoke excellent English, and she could understand him perfectly. He asked her to lie flat on her back on the examination table and pull down her jeans. He palpated her abdomen gently at first, with each push asking if she felt any pain. Next he pressed slowly and deliberately in one spot, his palms overlapping slightly, then released the pressure rapidly. Isobel let out a yelp of pain.

"You can sit up now," he said, wiping his hands with disinfectant. "You have acute appendicitis. The blood test shows an infection, and on the ultrasound there is fluid around your appendix, which is enlarged. We will need to do a laparoscopic surgery and probably remove your appendix. If you agree, we will do this just as soon as I can find a bed for you. Until then we will start you on intravenous antibiotics."

Isobel nodded mechanically. All she wanted was for the pain to go away.

"I have to warn you that because you are pregnant, there

may be complications." His eyes met hers. "You understand what I am saying?"

"What? You're saying I'm pregnant?"

"Yes. You did not know? It's routine for us to check with a woman of childbearing age. The blood test was positive, and the ultrasound also shows it. You conceived about twelve weeks ago."

Chapter 27

Isobel sat in the waiting area, a bag of clear fluid dripping into an intravenous port taped to the back of her hand. The pain was all encompassing, obliterating any rational thought. When she caught the attention of a nurse, she pointed to her side, grimaced, and mimed swallowing a pill. The woman just shook her head, then tapped at her watch. For the next two hours people came and went, but Isobel hardly noticed. She felt like a ghost, existing in a different dimension. A different nurse came to change her drip, and Isobel roused herself briefly to inquire about going to the toilet. The nurse disconnected the IV line and pointed to a nearby door. Entering the toilet, she went through the motions mechanically, then offered her hand to be re-connected to her tether when she returned to her seat in the waiting area. Pain had become her only thought. Everything else would have to wait.

Yet another nurse, this one wearing a gown and mask and pushing a wheelchair. emerged from the elevator at the other end of the corridor. She approached, stopping every so often to talk with members of the staff, one of whom pointed to

Isobel. She parked the wheelchair in front of Isobel and said something in Italian, but seeing the look of incomprehension, gestured for Isobel to sit while she disconnected the IV line. Hoisting Isobel's pack on her shoulder, she pushed the wheelchair with one hand and dragged the roll-on bag with the other. The elevator lurched downward before opening into a brightly lit, long corridor that reminded Isobel of scenes in sci-fi movies where the victim is wheeled away to their fate. *If I keep my eyes tightly closed, none of this is really happening, and when I open them again, I'll be at home.*

～

She opened her eyes and looked around. She was in a hospital room, lying on a bed beside a swing-out tray. She was warm and comfortable and miraculously, felt no pain. Her mouth was dry, and she licked her lips. A familiar face appeared — her surgeon — flanked by two white-coated young men. The threads of the past came back in small pieces, gradually assembling into something recognizable. This was the man who had told her she was going to have her appendix removed. This was the man who told her.... She forced her mind to avoid that icy sliver of memory as if, by doing so, it would melt and disappear. Her surgeon was saying something to her. He spoke slowly and deliberately while she tried to concentrate on what he was saying.

"The surgery was successful. We made three small incisions and removed your appendix which was perforated. It had adhered to the wall of the cecum, which was also necrotic. We had to remove a small piece of the cecum too."

He mimed the procedure with his hands, but seeing incomprehension on Isobel's face, he gestured for a piece of paper and proceeded to draw an outline of the digestive system, pointing to the appendix and cecum.

"This is where I removed the diseased tissue — just a small piece, near the junction with the colon. It is closed with staples. The staples will remain. The three incisions are closed with sutures, and these will be removed in about ten days. You should have no problems with your pregnancy."

The words poured over and around her.

"Water," she mumbled, licking at her dry lips.

"Later," came his response.

The surgical entourage left, and she lay there quietly, allowing random thoughts to filter in and out. What was it he had said? The surgery went well. Something about needing to remove part of the cecum. She struggled to remember the anatomy of the digestive system. Wasn't the cecum where the appendix was attached? He had said something else, something about pregnancy. The memory arrived with the ferocity of a tornado. She had been pregnant. No. She was *still* pregnant. The surgery had not interfered with that. She closed her eyes, begging sleep to come.

Chapter 28

Isobel stayed in the Borgo Trento hospital for five more days. Unlike the United States, where cost dictated a rapid discharge after a surgery such as this, in Italy there was no need to hurry. True, hospital beds were always in short supply. But Isobel had been told this was a recently built surgical wing that added almost two hundred beds to the original hospital. Moreover, she was in a teaching hospital where trainee doctors were plentiful. They came to rounds, each of them anxious to discuss her treatment and recovery and at the same time practice their English. Had she not been dealing with an existential crisis, she might have appreciated their participation, especially as she had recently been preparing for a career in veterinary medicine. But there was no ignoring the reality of her situation. She was in a hospital where few of the nursing staff spoke English, recovering from a surgery that involved more than just taking out a ruptured appendix. Part of her intestine had been infected and in removing it the surgeon had warned her there was a risk of further infection, blood clots, and bleeding.

The possibility of a second surgery was not ruled out; he would know more in a day or two when she started to eat solid food.

Initially, Isobel had hoped she would have a private room, but sharing had distinct advantages. Her neighbor, Sofia, spoke a little English. She was recovering from a collapsed lung but nonetheless was allowed to get out of bed and walk around the hospital. When Isobel needed to get her phone and the charging cable from the locker where her luggage had been stowed, Sofia obliged, plugging it into a charging port on the wall whenever that was needed.

Isobel thought about the conversation she was going to have with Vic. She wrestled with how much to tell him. One part of her yearned to see him. But then what? There was nothing he could do for her here. Hospital visitors were restricted to an hour at noon and again in the evening. What would he do to occupy himself during the daytime? Even though Verona was known as a beautiful and romantic destination, Vic didn't speak Italian and was unlikely to be interested in the city's tourist offerings. He would become frustrated and resentful, knowing that his work projects were lying idle back in Wisconsin. No. Vic was definitely not coming to Italy. She would reassure him that the operation had gone smoothly, the hospital was excellent, and that she would be able to come home very soon. In her heart she knew this was what he wanted to hear.

She decided not to tell Vic about the pregnancy. This was her dilemma, and she needed time to think things through before deciding what to do. There was still a risk of a second, more invasive surgery, which might well end the pregnancy. She understood what a bowel resection involved and the prolonged recovery after such a surgery. If that happened, she definitely *would* want someone to come to Verona. But who? The first person she thought of was her mother. It took her by surprise that she would want Christina, but the past few weeks had given her a glimpse of a very different person than the one she remembered from her childhood. Had her father not been so ill, she might have asked her mother to come. Even with the ten thousand dollars she had loaned to Vic, there was still enough money to pay for a flight from New Zealand. Who then? Stan perhaps? Isobel laughed inwardly at the thought of Stan barging into her hospital room, chiding her for getting sick, then taking over. Her *moko* would intimidate doctors and nurses alike.

She spent the next hour composing an email to Vic. He would read it when he came home that evening, too late to call her. She had written that the hospital discouraged phone calls as they disturbed the other patients.

~

The first night was interrupted by a nurse coming to take a blood sample, and Isobel found it hard to get back to sleep. She lay awake for a few hours, wrestling with the question of how to contact Toma. For years she had thought of him as her *real* father, but since New Zealand that had changed. Novak was her true father, the person who had been there throughout her childhood. Despite everything she had learned about him, Toma was, for all intents and purposes, a stranger, and her affection for him was guarded. True, he had rescued her from Sarajevo, but he had made no effort to find her after the war. That was unforgivable. And now he was calling himself by another name, Paolo Parma, diminishing her attachment to him even more.

Early the next morning her team of doctors came by. They informed her that her recovery was going well but that she would be on a diet of liquid or semisolid food for one day at least. Her breakfast tray arrived soon afterwards — a disappointment, but nonetheless she devoured everything on it. Sofia had mentioned there was a café downstairs in the hospital atrium and a gift shop selling newspapers and books. Isobel asked her to find out if they sold cards and stamps. She returned with both, adding that there was a mailbox in the atrium where mail was collected at noon each day, and that she would be happy to go back and mail the card.

It took Isobel barely five minutes to write the card to Toma. The major points she wanted to get across were that she, Isobel Babić, was his daughter. She had come to Verona hoping to meet him but had ended up in hospital and was now recovering from an appendectomy. She gave him her room number at the hospital and added her cell phone number and email address. Sofia took the card to the mailbox, leaving Isobel to wonder if it would be delivered before she was discharged.

As the day progressed, she checked her email frequently, hoping to see something from Vic. Leaving the hospital was not going to be easy, and she wondered whether discouraging Vic from coming to Italy had been a good idea after all. All the medical websites she searched warned that it was not a good idea to fly after a surgery, which meant she would have to stay in Verona until her sutures were removed and she was cleared to travel. Those same websites also warned about not lifting anything that weighed more than ten pounds for the first couple of weeks. As a young and healthy female, she was inclined to interpret such medical advice loosely. Dragging a roll-on bag was not lifting, and she could transfer a few things from her backpack to her suitcase before she left the hospital. She'd manage. Next came the challenge of finding a place to stay when she left the hospital. Searching online, she found an inexpensive hotel within a ten-minute walk, Hotel Italia. To her relief the receptionist spoke perfect English, and Isobel explained her situation. The receptionist assured her they would have a room, and she could stay for as long as she needed.

Isobel knew she was using these problem-solving exercises to avoid thinking about the pregnancy. They allowed her to feel she was still in control. Meanwhile, another part of her brain was going through a parallel process of problem-solving while she avoided paying attention to it. Not yet, at least. Only when she was discharged from hospital would the pregnancy become real. By then it would be thirteen weeks. Add to that another week at a hotel in Verona before she could fly, and.... She deliberately shut down that line of thought. There was still time to decide.

Chapter 29

Vic's email was obviously written in haste as there were spelling mistakes and words missing. He was rushing to meet a client, he wrote, but would call Isobel just as soon as the meeting was finished. Surely the hospital staff would understand and make an exception, he wrote. She was a foreigner after all and with nobody there to help her. Isobel calculated that he would call midafternoon. That gave her a little time to marshal her arguments that he should absolutely *not* come to Verona. She explained the situation to Sofia, who offered to leave the room just as soon as the call came.

When her phone rang, Isobel was ready.

"Are you all right? Did the surgery go okay? What did the doctors say? I can't believe it, Isobel. Did you know something was wrong before you left here? A pain in your side or anything?"

The words tumbled over themselves, and it was reassuring to hear his voice, even if he sounded distraught.

"Vic, I'm fine. Honestly. It's all over now...well, at least I think it is. We'll see tomorrow or the day after if I can digest solid food. Once that's working, I'll be able to leave the hospital and come home." She hoped she sounded convincing.

"I could always come..." His voice trailed off. "I checked and my passport is still valid. I could easily find someone to look after Oliver for a few days."

Isobel interrupted him. "Vic, there's no need for you to come," she said and moved quickly to her arguments. "Of course I'd love to have you here, but it would be a waste of your time. First of all, I'll be in hospital for another four days. It's not like America. They don't chuck you out. They make sure you are fully healthy before they let you leave."

She heard an intake of breath from Vic, preparatory to his speaking.

"Listen to me. I am in good hands. It's a big teaching hospital just like in Madison, and everyone I've interacted with has been great."

"I don't want you to have to go through this alone."

Isobel sighed. If he only knew.

"I know that. But you wouldn't be able to help me here. They only allow visitors for an hour at noon and again in the evening. What would you do the rest of the time? And you don't speak Italian. That's one thing that's surprised me — most of the staff here don't speak English, only the doctors." She gave a little laugh. "I know you. You'd be frustrated. Your clients would hate you, and I'd end up worrying about you more than myself. That's not the best scenario for a speedy recovery, is it?"

She paused for a moment, wondering if her carefully rehearsed speech was making any impact.

"And then there's the whole business with Lara. That needs to be dealt with, and you can't do it from here."

The previous night she had spent several hours brooding

over Lara. Had it been a mistake to seek her out? After all, the woman was now becoming a thorn in Vic's side. At the time Isobel had been so proud of her sleuthing skills for finding Maggie's daughter had not been easy. She had reached out to a friend in Massachusetts, giving her Maggie's name, the name of the hospital where Lara was born together with the date of birth. They were likely breaking the law, but Isobel would have done anything for Maggie. The hospital had a busy gynecology unit, and there were several possibilities. Isobel had written to as many of them as she could find addresses for. Only one woman had answered, claiming she was Lara.

She could hear Vic's breathing, his exhale growing steadily louder until it reached the final crescendo of a sigh.

"Damn it, Isobel. You're right, but I feel like a jerk."

"Look, I know you want to help. But this is one of those times when you are better off concentrating on all the things you need to do at home. Don't worry about me. I'll be lying here in the lap of luxury." She giggled and was reassured to hear a snort of laughter from Vic.

"You're right. I suppose I wouldn't be much use to you there."

They chatted about Oliver for a few minutes, a safe topic as far as Isobel was concerned.

"He comes to Maggie's place with me all the time. I'm doing a lot of work there in the evenings, so if you try to call the landline at our place, I might not pick up."

"Don't worry. I'll email you."

One part of her wanted to keep talking, but another part wanted to quit the conversation while it was going her way.

"Oops. I've got to go. A nurse has just come in, and she's giving me a look that definitely says 'no telephone.'"

The call ended, and Isobel lay back on the pillows and

closed her eyes, confident she had played her part well. What would have happened had she told him she was pregnant? She honestly didn't know. Her mind went back to those times when she had called their landline and got no response. Was he really spending all his evenings at Maggie's house? Maybe something else was going on? Initially she had dismissed the possibility that Vic could be having an affair, but since Kauri, she realized how easy it was to seek solace in someone else's arms.

"Maggie, what would you do?"

The internal voice that answered was not Maggie but her mother.

The only important question is this: Do you want to be a mother?

Chapter 30

Sofia's family members usually came during the noon-to-one o'clock visiting hour, so when a man appeared at the door of their room two days later, Isobel smiled briefly and returned to the book she had downloaded on her computer.

"Isobel Babić," the man said with a catch in his breath. He stared at her, his eyes exploring her face and taking in every detail.

The man was tall, a little over six feet, with unconventionally long hair transitioning to gray. The trimmed beard and moustache confirmed he had once been blond. She guessed he was in his mid-fifties.

"I'm Paolo Parma," he said, approaching her bed.

He smiled, and for an instant Isobel could see the resemblance to Novak. She stared at him for what seemed like an eternity, her mouth open, as if to speak but suddenly struck dumb.

Finally, she managed to utter a single word. "Toma?"

He nodded but repeated his original introduction, "Paolo

Parma," with some emphasis. His eyes shifted rapidly to the other bed. Sofia had resumed reading and was ignoring them.

Toma moved a chair close to her bed and sat down with his back to Sofia.

"Sorry. My English is not very good. Your card; it arrived today. I came immediately to see you. This is a surprise, no?"

With a few moments to regain her composure, Isobel responded with a dry laugh.

"You're telling me! I mean..." Her voice trailed off. Her mind was a blur as she tried to organize her thoughts into a coherent sentence.

"I don't know where to start," she said, shaking her head.

"I tried to find you in Canada. I tried to find Novak."

He seemed about to say something more, and she waited, every nerve in her body tensed. Then he shrugged, raising his hands in a gesture of defeat.

"I...I did not know what else to do."

He looked as if he were memorizing every feature of her face. She watched his eyes leaving hers, moving from forehead to cheeks to nose and mouth, then returning to her eyes.

"You look so much like Amela."

As if on cue to disrupt the moment, Isobel's lunch arrived. A clatter of metal on metal as the trolley banged against the door frame, followed by an irritated exclamation in Italian. Toma stood up abruptly.

"I will come back later. I will call your *telefonino*."

He turned his back on the orderly, who was occupied with delivering Sofia's lunch tray, and left the room. Isobel didn't know quite how to interpret his abrupt departure. Had he changed his mind about reconnecting with his daughter? Or was it as simple as that he needed to go to the bathroom urgently? Stunned, she ate the piece of boiled chicken on her plate together with a little pasta, hardly noticing what she was putting in her mouth.

"Was that the person you sent the card to?" Sofia asked companionably when they had finished their lunch. "A friend?"

Isobel was about to say "That was my father," but changed her mind. Something about Toma's insistence on calling himself Paolo, of avoiding both Sofia and the orderly, had put her on alert.

"Not exactly. Just someone whose name and address I was given by a friend because I was coming to Verona."

Sofia seemed to accept this explanation for she just nodded, adding, "It is good you have someone here in Verona to help you."

Shortly after lunch Sofia went down to the atrium to get some exercise. Left alone, Isobel thought about her visitor. She hadn't expected to meet her father in these circumstances. She would have preferred a meeting over coffee or lunch, with people around to provide a neutral backdrop. That was how Maggie had arranged to meet her daughter the previous year, rather than inviting Lara to her cabin. At the time Isobel had wondered why. Now she understood — these meetings were potential minefields.

Isobel dragged her thoughts back to the present. Novak had been right. Despite a somewhat weather-beaten face, Toma was exceedingly handsome, but unlike his brother, he had penetrating green-brown eyes. Isobel's eyes were blue; even so, she thought she saw something of herself in his face. The cheekbones perhaps or maybe it was the shape of her mouth. She mulled over what he had said, that she looked like Amela. Gordana had said the same thing. With all her heart Isobel wished there could be another miracle, but whereas Toma's resurrection was plausible, her mother's was not.

The following afternoon one of the young doctors who spoke excellent English — he had spent a year at a hospital in Yorkshire — came to tell her that as she was tolerating food well, she would be released the following day. The news was welcome but at the same time disturbing. The days in hospital had provided her with an excuse to avoid facing up to the rest of her life. Now she would have to make some critical decisions.

Chapter 31

Isobel's phone rang the following morning as she was getting ready to leave the hospital. It was Toma, wanting to know if he could visit her again. She told him she was moving to Hotel Italia on Via Mameli where she planned to stay for another week before returning to the United States.

"I can drive you there," he offered.

She considered for a moment. It wasn't exactly how she planned to meet her father again. Nonetheless it would simplify getting to the hotel and save her having to ask someone to call for a taxi. She accepted his offer, and they agreed she would call him when she was about to leave. He gave her his number, and she entered it into her contacts, scrolling down to the letter P for Parma, not B for Babić.

No lunch tray was delivered, which she interpreted as a good sign. Shortly after lunch her surgeon came to the room, a sheaf of papers in his hand. He explained that they were in Italian, but if she had any questions, there was a number she could call. He pointed to a couple of lines on the second page showing two upcoming appointments, the first to have her stitches removed, the second to get final approval to travel. By then, he assured her, the pathology report would be available, although he stressed that he didn't think there would be anything of significance in it. Finally, he offered to refer her to the Mother and Children's Hospital if she wished to make an appointment.

"They can help you with any decision," he added, a neutral expression on his face.

His offer was something she hadn't expected, and in a different situation she might have welcomed the opportunity to talk things over with a professional counselor. But the challenge of having to explain her conflicted feelings to someone who might not speak English fluently, let alone understand the issues associated with unscheduled pregnancy in the United States, was daunting. She declined, saying she planned to fly home just as soon as she got the all clear from the surgical team. She thanked him sincerely for his excellent care, complimented his colleagues and the hospital staff, and shook hands with him.

When the surgeon had gone, Isobel took off her hospital gown and dressed slowly. She wasn't worried about damaging her stitches but rather the staples in her large intestine. Unlike skin, the large intestine could easily tear if she exerted herself too much. Sofia carried her luggage to the main entrance where they said their goodbyes. Then she called Toma's number.

"I am there in twenty...thirty minutes. My car is an old Toyota Land Cruiser. Big. Easy to recognize." He sounded pleased.

Fortunately, there was a bench in front of the hospital entrance where she could sit and wait because, despite walking around her hospital floor, she had not been very active for the past six days and felt a little unsteady. She'd lost weight and her jeans were looser than when she had last worn them. Now that she was moving around, her breasts felt tender. She had first noticed this in New Zealand, but at the time had blamed it on carrying a backpack. Never once had she considered she might be pregnant. True, her period had been spotty, but she had blamed that on the stress of Maggie's death and her decision to go to New Zealand. According to the websites she consulted for what to expect in the first trimester, she was among twenty percent of lucky women who didn't experience morning sickness. And now she was crossing the threshold of the second trimester. She pushed the thought aside.

~

The Toyota was easy to spot as it approached the hospital entrance. Toma pulled up beside the bench and jumped out to get her luggage, which he put into the back of the vehicle. He held the front passenger door open but avoided touching her as she climbed cautiously up into the seat.

"The hotel is very close," he said, then fell silent.

Isobel didn't feel like talking either. She wanted to see the route they were taking because, if for some reason she had to return to the hospital, she needed to know where to find it. She smiled briefly at the absurdity of her situation. Thus far she had seen nothing of Verona, known the world over as the setting for Shakespeare's *Romeo and Juliet,* and there was little chance she would.

They parked in front of the hotel, and Toma walked around to open the passenger door, this time offering his hand. She took it, briefly.

"Would you mind bringing in my bags?" she asked. "I'm not allowed lift more than... 'em, four kilos."

"Yes, I understand." He nodded, holding open the door that led into the hotel.

At the reception desk, Isobel presented her passport and a credit card. With the formalities completed, she turned to Toma, who stood beside her luggage in the foyer.

"Thank you so much," she said, not sure what to do or say next. "I can get someone to take the luggage to my room."

"Please. I'll take it."

With a nod, she acquiesced. After all, this man *was* her father. The tiny elevator felt crowded with just the two of them, and she was glad when it stopped at her floor. She found her room and unlocked the door. Stepping aside, she allowed Toma to push it open and take her luggage inside. He placed her suitcase on a luggage stand and her backpack beside the bed.

"You will be okay now?" he asked.

"Yes. I'll be fine," she assured him.

She was exhausted both emotionally and physically. All she wanted to do was to lie down and close her eyes.

"Tomorrow would you like to have dinner with me? The restaurant here at the hotel, it is a nice place to talk. No?"

He was right. They needed to talk, and the restaurant would be as good a place as any.

"Yes. I would like that. We'll talk." She smiled weakly.

"Seven o'clock?"

"Yes. Seven o'clock."

With a tiny hesitation, he stepped forward and kissed her on both cheeks. Then he left, closing the door behind him quietly. She lay down on the bed but found it impossible to relax. Unlike the hospital, with endless interruptions that broke the monotony, here she was alone with her thoughts, and in particular with the one thought she had managed to keep at bay thus far. Did she want to have a baby? In Wisconsin six weeks ago, the answer would have been an emphatic no. She had plans for her future, her career as a veterinarian, and they didn't include a child. But something had changed in New Zealand. What was it? She searched her mind for an answer but nothing satisfied. Gradually, she fell into a light sleep, aroused occasionally by doors opening and closing in the corridor as other guests used their rooms.

Waking an hour later, she shivered a little and pulled the duvet over her. The last wisp of a dream was fading but not before leaving a lingering image of a young woman with a baby. At first, she thought the young woman must be Amela. But no. The baby had been suckling at Isobel's breast.

Chapter 32

The problem with time zones, whether in New Zealand or Italy, was that there never was a good time to call Vic. Seven hours, seventeen hours — it hardly mattered. Either he was on a job site and under pressure or he was working at Maggie's cabin. By now she had dismissed any suspicions that he was having an affair. Those late nights and weekends at the cabin had an element of obsession about them, as if he were trying to make amends for not having discovered Maggie in time. The lawyer's letter with Lara's accusation was adding even more stress to his life, and Isobel's conversations with him were never relaxed. For Vic, the only way to deal with problems was to knuckle down and work even harder, filling every spare moment with something physically demanding to distract and exhaust him. Had she been there, Isobel knew she would be able to talk him into a reasonable frame of mind. Instead, when she pictured him at home, he wore a perpetual frown instead of a smile.

Maggie's cabin had been Isobel's favorite place in the world until Maggie's death. She had spent countless hours there while she was working for Maggie, coming to accept the shortcomings of a building that had been hastily constructed by settlers in the middle of the 1800s. Maggie had bought the cabin and the surrounding land when she first arrived in Wisconsin to work at the university and had lived there for fifty years. Little had changed over that period besides necessary repairs and the addition of a screened-in porch. The porch was where she had read Maggie's letters aloud to her, hearing in them the voice of a young woman struggling to make her way in a new country, narrating a tale of excitement, new friendships, and success. Much later, Maggie had admitted to Isobel what lay between those carefully crafted lines — a distraught young woman, pregnant, and with no place to turn.

Isobel wasn't sure she wanted Vic to alter the cabin in any way, but it was not her decision. Maggie had left it to him. It was true the kitchen needed some work. For several months after Maggie's fall, Isobel had prepared meals in that kitchen, so she was intimate with its shortcomings and idiosyncrasies. The floor sagged in one spot and a person was likely to fall through at some future time, as the kitchen had no real foundation. With winter approaching, there had been no time for the newly arrived immigrants from Switzerland to dig a basement. Instead, a layer of fresh cut logs had been laid directly on the sandy ground under the kitchen floor. Maggie had replaced the windows and the sliding glass door that led onto the deck. Nonetheless, the room was always either too hot in summer or too cold in winter. Isobel smiled to herself, remembering how she and Maggie would sit at the kitchen table over endless cups of tea discussing Isobel's hopes and dreams. It was ironic that now she too was alone in a foreign country, and pregnant.

She waited until close to midnight to call Vic. He picked up the phone after two rings.

"Does this mean you are out of hospital?" he asked without preamble. "Are you okay? How are you feeling?"

"I got out this afternoon, and I'm now at the hotel. I sent you all the information in my last email — Hotel Italia. It's fairly near the hospital, in case anything goes wrong. It's comfortable enough, considering I'm going to be stuck here for the next week or so. At least it's got its own restaurant.

"Is that what the doctors told you, a week before you can travel?"

"Yeah. I know it's a long time, but they are very thorough here. As soon as I get the all-clear from them, I'll book a flight."

"I could still come, you know. We could hang out together. It wouldn't be much of a vacation, but I'd be able to look after you. You must be lonely." He paused before adding, "I'm lonely too."

"Honestly, there's no point in you coming. I can't do much walking so you'd just be hanging around the hotel with me, both of us bored and liable to get on each other's nerves. This way you get some work done, and I get to take it easy. I've got my computer so I can catch up with emails, read, even watch movies. They've got good internet here at the hotel. I'm always complaining I never have enough time for that sort of stuff at home." She chuckled. "I can binge on the latest Netflix drama."

"It must have been awful to be in hospital and not able to speak the language. I don't know how you did it."

Isobel could hear the relief in Vic's voice and made an effort to sound upbeat.

"Actually, it wasn't so bad. I had Sofia, and I got very good at using Google Translate."

They chatted briefly about the work he was doing at Maggie's house.

"Oliver seems to have gotten over Maggie not being there. I mean, he doesn't charge upstairs to her bedroom anymore. He's happy enough to lie on the kitchen floor and keep me company unless I'm making too much noise. Then he goes into the front room and climbs up on the couch. I know you never let him do that, but…"

He laughed and she joined in. It felt good to hear a lightness in his voice for a change.

"Did you get the money?" she asked.

"Yes. And I really appreciate it. You know I'll pay you back, but it takes a load of stress off to know I can pay this lawyer. He's drafting a response to Lara's last accusations, which he says are totally bogus. I know they are. It'll never get to court, but it's going to take a lot of money and time for this to be finally settled."

Isobel's thoughts had shifted to Toma — Paolo — and how to introduce this new piece of information into their conversation. One part of her didn't want to say anything about her father just now. She wasn't sure how she felt about him. At the same time, she wanted to shout from the rooftops that she had finally met her *real* father, seen him in the flesh, even recognized herself in his features. She decided to keep it to herself a little longer. After she and Toma had dinner the following evening, she would have a lot more to tell Vic.

Chapter 33

Isobel picked up a guidebook from a table in the hotel lobby and brought it to the dining room the following morning. From a corner table she watched the guests, many of them tourists, lingering over their breakfasts while they planned a day of sightseeing. A few tapped on their computers while they ate, presumably preparing for a day of business. She had slept fairly well, although going to the bathroom during the night had been a reminder that she had only Tylenol for the pain and not something stronger. There were many places in the city she would have enjoyed seeing, but they were too far from the hotel for her to walk, and she felt secure being close to the hospital. Perhaps later in the week she would take a taxi to the Roman arena or the Cathedral of San Zeno, the patron saint of the city. And then there was Juliet's House, not the original, of course, but the guidebook said it was a Verona must-see nonetheless.

After almost a week in hospital, even walking around the immediate neighborhood gave her a sense of freedom. Traffic was relatively light on the streets, which were bordered by mature trees shading the elegant Liberty-style palazzos. It was easy to find a place to sit and rest; every street corner seemed to have a café or bistro that served a perfect cappuccino.

The upcoming dinner with Toma was forefront in her mind that morning. With the exception of their shared DNA, he was no different from any stranger she might pass on the street, yet their conversation would be very different. Where to begin? She struggled to identify what was really important. She knew about his childhood from her conversation with Novak. She didn't want to get into his politics or what he did in the war. At least not yet. What she really wanted to know was how he and her mother had met, how they had fallen in love. What was Amela like? Was she athletic? Did she like to read or prefer to go dancing? These were the easy questions. There were others, and she was determined by the end of the evening to get answers. Why had he not spirited Amela out of Sarajevo? Why had he not tried harder to find his daughter?

∼

Toma was waiting for her in the lobby when she came down from her room at seven that evening. She had taken a much-needed nap in the afternoon, but even though she felt rested, she was apprehensive about the evening, her stomach slightly nauseous. Toma escorted her to the restaurant, and they sat at a table in a quiet corner. Neither of them seemed ready to embark on a weighty conversation, and instead they talked about the Borgo Trento neighborhood and its architecture. When the waiter came to their table, Toma questioned him in rapid-fire Italian before making a choice. Isobel ordered a pasta dish, the name of which she recognized on the menu. It would be far better than anything she had eaten in the hospital where the food had been surprisingly insipid.

"I want to show you a photograph," Toma said. A muscle in his cheek twitched momentarily as he waited for her response.

"Sure. Go ahead."

He reached into his jacket pocket and pulled out a postcard-sized photograph, which he passed over to her. She took it, noting how the edges were frayed as if it had been handled many times.

"It's Amela and me before the war."

For several minutes Isobel stared at the photograph. Here they were at last, her *real* parents. They looked like any young couple happy and in love. He had his arm around her; she had turned slightly to look up into his face. Both of them were smiling as if they didn't have a care in the world.

"I cannot give it to you. It is the only photograph I have of us together. Do you have your telefonino? You could take a picture of it."

"You were right. We do look alike," Isobel said. "She's prettier than me though."

Carefully, she positioned the photograph on the table and pulled out her phone. Standing up, she leaned over, making sure the image was square in the screen, then took several shots.

"Thank you for bringing it," she said. "Gordana has no photos of...my mother. She told me she lost all of her things in the war."

Their meal arrived soon afterwards, and they both said little while eating. As soon as Isobel had finished, Toma sat back in his chair as if he had been waiting for this moment. She sensed his impatience.

"Tell me about your life in North America," he said without preamble.

The directness of his request took her aback. She began to talk, tentatively at first, but gradually enjoying recounting this paraphrased edition of her life: childhood, adolescence, teenage years, tennis, college in the United States, working as a school counselor in Madison. The only time he interrupted her narrative was when she mentioned being a school counselor. There didn't seem to be an equivalent in Italian schools, although that might have been the description Isobel gave of her previous job. She told him about her decision to become a vet, her acceptance to veterinary school, and finally the windfall from Maggie that had enabled her to go to New Zealand to see her parents.

"Novak and Christina live in New Zealand?" He looked stunned.

"Yes. They moved there the first year I was in college. It was a shock to me too, but Mom's from New Zealand, and she wanted to go back there. They ran a bed-and-breakfast for a few years on North Island, but then Dad got sick so they moved to South Island. They live in a place called Motueka. "

She was about to continue, but Toma interrupted her.

"Novak is sick? What is wrong with him?" He was frowning now.

Something snapped inside her. This man who barely two days ago had appeared in her life was now concerned about his family?

Her eyes blazing, she snarled at him. "He's got cancer, and he's never going to get better and..." She fought back tears. "Dad never told me he was really my uncle. I only found out two weeks ago. They told me I was adopted, but they wouldn't tell me anything else. Just that I had been born in Sarajevo. All of my life I believed I was abandoned by my real parents. Do you have any idea what that does to a person? Do you?"

For a long time Toma just looked at her, not saying anything, his mask-like expression betraying nothing. When he finally spoke, he averted his eyes.

"Amela did *not* abandon you. She was killed."

"But *you* did." Isobel jabbed her finger towards him.

"I suppose you could look at it that way. But what could I have done with a baby? There was a war going on. I couldn't go to Sarajevo. At least I managed to get you out of there, get you safely to Canada where I knew Novak would take care of you."

She waited for him to say something more, to offer her a better excuse.

"I am a different person now."

They sat in an uneasy silence.

"Why didn't you get my mother out of Sarajevo? If you got me out, why not her?"

"She refused to leave. Sarajevo was her home. She grew up there, went to university, had friends, a good job. I told her to go, go anywhere. I told her I could help her get out of the city. But she wouldn't."

"Couldn't she have gone to live with you?"

Toma made to reply, then stopped. He raised his hands, palms upward.

"You cannot understand." His forehead creased as he searched for words. "Nobody understands. In Sarajevo back then everyone belonged to an ethnic group. Me, I was a Serbian Orthodox Christian. Amela was a Bosnian Muslim. We loved each other, but we could never be married. It was not possible in Sarajevo then."

Isobel found herself glancing at his left hand, which was resting on the table. He was wearing a wedding ring.

"I joined a group of Serbs who believed in a Greater Serbia, a place where no one would be treated badly just for being Serb. I believed in the cause and was willing to fight for it, willing to do just about anything. Novak disagreed with me. He thought..., well, I'm not sure what he thought. He and I got into terrible fights, and then he went to Canada. I was seventeen at the time. Our mother had died a couple of years before of cancer. Maybe she could have prevented our falling out had she lived, maybe not."

This was one of the questions Isobel hadn't had a chance to ask Novak. Listening to his brother now, she wondered how he might have answered it. He must have forgiven his little brother. Why else did he agree to adopt her? Her heart ached that she would never see Novak again. She turned her attention back to Toma, trying to focus on the fact that, while this man was her biological father, she didn't feel drawn to him in any way. He continued talking, and she realized he was trying to justify his actions.

"Once the war started, it wasn't easy for Amela and me to see each other. We couldn't meet openly. I would have been killed by Muslim extremists or captured by the Bosnian army. After all, my Serbian comrades were shelling the city."

Isobel had heard enough. She didn't care about his excuses. She wanted to run from the room and never see him again. Instead, she forced herself to speak, her tone ice cold.

"Your brother, who took me in and brought me up and was kind to me, my *true* father is dying. You should go and see him. He deserves that much from you."

She could see Toma looking at her, searching for a shred of understanding or forgiveness. She stared back at him with hate in her eyes.

"I don't think Novak wants to see me. I wrote to him.... It was six years ago. I wanted us to be reconciled. I wanted to know about you. He never replied."

"He couldn't," Isobel said, shaking her head, "He never got your letter. They had moved to New Zealand by then."

"I wrote to Gordana too, hoping she might know something about you, but she had lost contact with Novak."

"You and your stupid war messed up so many lives." Isobel spat the words out. "Dad wrote to Gordana a bunch of times during those first few years. He even sent pictures of me for her to pass on to you. But she never got the letters. The thing is, she didn't go back to Sarajevo after Canada, she went to Padua and stayed there until the war was over." Isobel gave a little shrug. "Dad made inquiries after the war and was told you were dead. It was only when I met Gordana a week ago that I found out you were still alive. She told me about my mother, how she died." Isobel began to cry, indifferent to the tears streaming down her face and dripping onto the tablecloth.

"It's all so fucking sad."

She got up from the table and left the room.

CHAPTER 34

Throwing herself onto the bed, Isobel curled into a fetal position and cried. Her abdomen ached, and her throat felt sore and scratchy. She hoped she wasn't getting the flu. Nothing had gone the way she expected, from the moment she left Wisconsin until now. It would be just her luck if she had to postpone going home for yet another week because of a stupid virus. She wanted someone to hold her, hug her, cradle her in their arms and reassure her everything was going to be all right. She thought of Vic, then Maggie, and finally her dad. He was the one she wanted right now. He would listen, hold her hand, and tell her everything was going to work out in the end. Emotionally drained, she fell into a deep sleep and was surprised to see sunlight filtering into the room through a gap in the drapes when she finally woke.

After breakfast she sat at her computer and typed a long email to Vic. He would be asleep and not get her message until later. Now she was ready to tell him everything about Toma from when he first appeared in her hospital room to their dinner last night. She typed furiously, pouring her anger and frustration into words. At the same time a part of her brain was trying to be more analytical, parsing each decision, each missed opportunity and failure to communicate. Everyone was culpable, Novak and Toma and Gordana, even Christina. She hated Toma for what he had done and what he had failed to do. But how could you hate a father you spent your life fantasizing about and hoping to find? He hadn't lived up to her expectations, and yet...he could have ignored her card and gone on with his life.

What had prompted Toma to contact Novak and Gordana six years ago, and why had he changed his name to Paolo Parma? She had an inkling as to the answer to the second question, but the first one still puzzled her. She threw these questions out in her email to Vic, hoping that with all the information she had provided, he might have some ideas. Hitting the send key on her computer, a wave of relief flooded over her. It felt good to share all of this with Vic.

∼

"You should go to San Zeno today," the woman at the reception desk suggested when Isobel came down to the lobby to get a cup of coffee.

"There's a market the first Sunday of every month in the square in front of the cathedral, a kind of flea market with stalls selling just about anything you can imagine. It's a lot of fun. Mostly it's locals who go. I think it might be a bit out of the way for tourists. There are cafés and restaurants, and people take their children and meet up with friends for lunch. You'll enjoy it, and if you are tired afterwards, you can always get a taxi back."

She handed Isobel a card with the name and phone number of a taxi company.

"Call this number and tell them where to pick you up. The dispatcher speaks English."

Back in her room, Isobel looked at a map of the city. San Zeno lay to the south of Borgo Trento, across the Adige River. It didn't look that far away, and the weather was perfect — a pleasant seventy degrees Fahrenheit, according to her phone.

So this is what it's like to be a tourist in Verona, Isobel thought as she crossed the arched Ponte di Castelvecchio a little while later. Street performers mingled with elderly strollers, Sunday bicyclists, young couples, families with children and dogs, all traversing the narrow pedestrian bridge. She stopped to look over the parapet, stepping up onto a stone plinth for a better view. In the river below were several inflatable boats, each filled with people wearing bright orange life jackets, all paddling towards a series of gentle rapids downstream. As she walked through the medieval city, she tried to imagine life in the time of Romeo and Juliet. It struck her that none of the challenges Toma and Amela had faced were new. Nor were her own. An unplanned pregnancy, an uncertain future, a father resurrected, a decision to be made.

In San Zeno she joined the swarm of people wandering through the square. There were hundreds of stalls, each with a miscellany of wares. Had she wanted, she could have bought a second-hand fur stole or a windup phonograph or a vintage medical illustration of the human body. By now her abdomen was hurting. Most of the park benches had been appropriated by the vendors, so she rested on the stone steps in front of the cathedral and watched the world spin around her. Children climbed on top of the two massive stone lions that flanked the entrance to the church, their joyful cries mingling with the hum of the crowd. She sat for a while taking in the vibrant scene, then moved to a restaurant around the corner from the cathedral, relieved to be able to sit in comfort. Around her people were drinking beer and wine with their meal, but she surprised herself by asking for a glass of sparkling water. After lunch she called for a taxi, giving the dispatcher the address on her receipt, and within ten minutes she was back at Hotel Italia.

Toma was waiting for her when she walked into the foyer. She wanted to ignore him and go straight to her room, but she didn't have the energy to argue when he blocked her way to the elevator.

"Please. I would like to ask you something."

She sat down carefully on the edge of a nearby sofa and sighed.

He was standing directly in front of her, close enough that she could smell his cologne.

"What do you want?" she asked coldly, looking up at him.

"I want to go to New Zealand to see my brother, and I want you to come with me."

She let the words sink in.

"I will pay everything. Please come with me."

Whether from fatigue or surprise, she was unable to form a coherent answer. Toma continued to stand above her, and for a moment she caught a glimpse of the dashing young student her mother had fallen in love with. But there was an element of foreboding about him too. He was a man accustomed to being obeyed.

When she didn't answer, he took a seat beside her. He offered to get her a coffee, a glass of water, but she shook her head. His hands were clasped on his lap as if in prayer. She noticed they were scarred, and the tip of one of the fingers on his right hand was missing. His hands reminded her of her dad's, which were also covered in scars from working on car engines. Her thoughts shifted to Novak, an image of him lying in a hospital bed looking gaunt, his life narrowing with each oxygen-enriched breath he took. Her dad was dying, and it was in her power to reunite him with his brother. Would it also be a reconciliation? She didn't know. But she had to try. She owed it, not to Toma, but definitely to her dad. And she would get to see him one more time.

"Let me think about it," she said, getting up from the sofa. "I'll call you tomorrow and let you know."

∼

That evening she ate alone at a pizzeria close to the hotel. It was the sort of place only locals knew about with simple, yet satisfying, food. After the meeting with Toma, she longed to order a half bottle of wine, but instead asked for water. She didn't try to analyze her abstemious choice. A large, multi-generational family entered while she was eating and fussed for several minutes as they took their places at a long table beside hers. She tensed with irritation, expecting the children to whine at their exhausted parents or take advantage of what were clearly their indulgent grandparents. Instead, the cacophony of cheerful voices raised her spirits. A tiny part of her wished she was sitting at their table.

∼

Telling Vic about her change of plans had been the start of an uncomfortable conversation. There was no way to soften the blow. She had hoped he would be happy she had finally met her biological father. Was he jealous perhaps? Up to now Vic had been the only man of consequence in her life. Now she had not one but two fathers, both alive, both taking up all of her emotional energy as well as her time, leaving nothing for Vic. Thinking about it that way, she couldn't really blame him.

"Why do you have to go with him to New Zealand in any case? Surely, he can get there by himself."

It was a question Isobel had asked herself. The prospect of another long plane journey was unappealing, and she had already said her goodbyes to Novak and Christina.

"I think he wants me to be there as a sort of buffer, in case Novak refuses to see him."

She heard Vic sigh.

"Think of it this way. It'll give me a chance to see Dad one more time. I feel badly that I left so quickly. They both understood why, but the goodbyes weren't easy. I'm still their daughter. I've grown up a lot since they left Canada, and we became much closer while I was in New Zealand. Now I understand how hard it was for them. I miss them. Both of them. Look, it'll only be another couple of weeks. By the time I get home, I'll have enough frequent flier miles for us to go anywhere we want, although I doubt I'll want to get on a plane for quite some time." She gave a chuckle.

Another silence, but she could sense Vic was coming around.

"Okay," he finally said. "I get it. And I'm sure your dad will appreciate everything you've done. It's kinda weird to think he hasn't seen his brother in more than thirty years. That's a lifetime."

There was a pause. Isobel could almost hear his brain processing the information.

"I suppose the trip will give you some time to get to know

the guy. He's your real dad after all. You both have a lot of catch-up to do."

Isobel changed the subject, certain the next topic would distract him.

"I've been thinking about Lara. Maybe it's because I'm not there, not wrapped up in it the way you are. But if you look at the situation critically, we only have her word for it that she's Maggie's daughter."

"What?" Vic said, a note of incredulity in his voice.

"What I'm trying to say is, Lara could be an imposter. She might have seen my letter as a way to get some money from an old lady who was looking for her long-lost daughter. I know it sounds horrible, but people do all sorts of things for money."

"But you're the one who found her. You're telling me you could have made a mistake?"

"Maybe. We don't have any proof she's Lara. There were eleven baby girls born in the hospital that day. My friend managed to track down seven of them, and that's who I wrote to. Grace Mangan was the only one who replied, so I automatically assumed she was Lara. I *wanted* her to be Lara, and I'm sure Maggie did too. But what if she isn't?"

"Mmm. How could we prove it?" Vic said, his tone suggesting that he was open to the idea.

"Remember I told you about Gordana, the lady I met in Sarajevo, the one who brought me to Canada? Well, she specializes in forensic genetics — identifying dead people from their remains. I was thinking, if we had Maggie's DNA, we could ask Grace Mangan to provide her DNA and compare the two."

"But how are we going to get Maggie's DNA? She was cremated."

"I was thinking about that. I didn't get around to cleaning out her bathroom before I left. I was too busy with everything else. Her toothbrush and hairbrush should still be there. I can check with Gordana, but I Googled it, and I'm pretty sure you can get DNA from a toothbrush or even hair. Can you ask your lawyer to formally request that Grace Mangan provide a sample of her DNA for testing? Even though I don't think she has a legal right to inherit, I'd prefer to know that it's Maggie's daughter we are dealing with and not a grifter."

"That's a really good idea. If the DNA doesn't match, that would put an end to the whole business, and I could stop worrying that Maggie's place could be taken away from me. You and I could move into the cabin and get on with our lives."

Chapter 35

Isobel had written a detailed email to Gordana, bringing her up to date with the reason she was still in Verona and how she had finally met Toma. Gordana replied immediately, expressing her delight. A day later she emailed Gordana again, this time with a very different agenda. As briefly as she could, she told the story of Maggie and her daughter Lara, how close Maggie and Vic had been, and how Maggie had signed her property over to Vic while she was still alive. Now Lara was claiming that the property had been given to Vic under duress.

> *Maybe it's because of everything I learned in the past few weeks, about my mother, about Toma and how he got me out of Sarajevo with false papers, how he managed to disappear and turn up later in Italy with a new identity... how you can pretend all sorts of stuff and get away with it. That got me thinking. What if this person calling herself Lara is a swindler preying on Vic and trying to get money under false pretenses? I've read that you can get a reliable sample of DNA from a toothbrush. If Vic sent you Maggie's*

toothbrush, would you be able to extract the DNA from it? If so, we could compare it with a sample from Lara and see if they match.

Gordana's reply came within an hour, reassuring Isobel that she and Vic might be able to put an end to the harassment. She suggested that Vic's lawyer be the one to collect Maggie's toothbrush. That way there would be fewer questions as to authenticity. She provided the name of a company in Madison who specialized in DNA testing. They would be able to do the test and also send a test kit to Lara's lawyer. Gordana offered to interpret the results, although the company would be able to do this too.

∼

Ever since the morning Isobel called Toma and agreed to go to New Zealand with him, they had had little contact. It was as if neither of them wanted to analyze the decision they had made, lest they acknowledge the magnitude of it and find an excuse to back out. As a condition of her going, Isobel had insisted Toma answer the question that had been puzzling her for days. Why the change of heart six years earlier when he wrote that letter to Gordana? His answer had surprised her.

"After the war I didn't think I was the sort of person who should be a father. You would have been five or six at that time. How could I take you away from Novak when I had nothing to offer? I was not a nice person."

"Oh," was all Isobel could find to say.

"I moved around for several years, eventually settling here in Verona. Eight years ago I met the woman who is now my wife. Then my son was born. That is when I realized how important family is. That is when I reached out to Gordana and to Novak. I wanted to find you."

Isobel felt her attitude towards him soften slightly. He had a son. This growing family of hers now included a half brother. The idea of a sibling gave her a little thrill.

~

They checked in separately at the Business Class desk at Milan Malpensa Airport. Isobel's ticket showed her return flight would be to the United States whereas Paolo Parma would be returning to Milan. The agent handed their passports back, together with their boarding passes, and directed each of them towards security.

"You go ahead of me," Toma said. "I need to go to the men's room. I'll meet you in the Emirates lounge in a few minutes."

She settled herself into a comfortable armchair in the lounge and was drinking a glass of sparkling water when Toma joined her.

"You don't much like flying, do you?" she asked innocently.

He gave her a sharp look.

"It's been a while since I flew anywhere. It's so easy to drive in Europe or take the train. I'm out of practice, I suppose."

"Not for me. It feels like I've spent weeks on airplanes recently. At least this trip isn't as long as the last one. Coming to Bosnia from New Zealand was endless.

"This is very nice." She gestured with her glass for emphasis. "Business class, I mean. I'll be able to sleep for most of the trip."

"It's only six hours to Dubai. Dubai to Auckland is the long one, sixteen hours."

"Yeah, but there are movies, and I've downloaded a couple of books."

The book Kauri had left for her was probably still in the waiting room at the Ljubljana bus terminal where she had thrown up. A pity, for she had been enjoying it.

"I told my wife about you." Toma's statement took her by surprise. He had a habit of being direct, as if small talk was a waste of his time.

"What do you mean?" she asked, frowning slightly.

"My wife, Francesca, knows very little about my past. She did not know I have a brother living in New Zealand," he hesitated, "or that I have a grown-up daughter living in America. I had to tell her these things because of this trip. She said she would like to meet you sometime." His voice dropped a notch. "She knows she will never meet my brother."

"And your son?"

"You would like him. He's almost seven." Toma smiled, and Isobel was again reminded of how good-looking he was.

"I didn't expect to have more children. But Francesca is quite a bit younger than me — fifteen years. She wanted a child."

"What's his name?"

"His name is Salvatore, but we call him Toto."

As if to discourage conversation, Toma had selected seats across the aisle from one another. Isobel ate very little of the meal and declined the wines on offer. She wondered if Toma had noticed. He probably thought she didn't especially like alcohol, which was so far from the truth. But time was moving forward inexorably, and she would have to make a decision soon. A few days earlier she had searched several websites to see whether a second trimester medical abortion was available in New Zealand. It would not be a problem.

During their three-hour layover in Dubai, they waited in the Emirates lounge. Unaccustomed to such luxury, Isobel remarked, "You must be very rich."

"I have a lot of money," Toma answered, his voice almost a whisper.

Her curiosity aroused, she probed further. "From the war?"

"Yes. And afterwards."

"Is that why you don't live in Bosnia now?" She hadn't wanted the question to sound confrontational.

"If I went back there today, I would be killed."

"By who? Bosniaks?"

In the past couple of days, Isobel had read as much as she could find on the breakup of Yugoslavia, the Bosnian War, and the ethnic groups that now dominated the different parts of Bosnia-Herzegovina. She had read that Bosniaks were a Slavic ethnic group comprised of mostly Muslim worshippers, some of whom were just as fervently nationalistic as their Serbian counterparts.

"By everyone," Toma said with finality.

∽

Just before they landed in Auckland, Toma leaned over to Isobel and whispered, "Once we land, we should act as if we do not know each other."

For a moment she considered asking why but quickly changed her mind. Their earlier conversation had left her with little doubt that her biological father had been a war profiteer, perhaps even worse.

In case she had any doubts, Toma continued, "I'm entering the country as Paolo Parma, an Italian tourist who wants to see where the *Lord of the Rings* movies were filmed. I have a ticket for a return flight in two weeks. You are an American citizen coming to visit your parents, who are citizens of New Zealand. Your father is sick."

She nodded.

"We will see each other in the arrivals hall after we clear immigration."

When they boarded the shuttle bus to the domestic terminal, Toma helped her with her suitcase. Isobel thanked him as she might a complete stranger, still not sure whether they were meant to be seen traveling together. He responded similarly. They didn't communicate again until their flight from Auckland arrived in Nelson, although Toma saw to it that she didn't have to lift her bag or backpack into the overhead bin in the plane.

"What's the plan now?" she asked once they had exited the terminal.

"I've rented a car and booked a hotel in Nelson for us for tonight. Tomorrow morning I want you to come with me to Motueka."

"You didn't tell them we were coming, did you." It was a statement rather than a question, and it struck Isobel that she had used a similar strategy the first time she came here. What other traits had she inherited from her biological father, she wondered?

"I was afraid if Novak knew my plans in advance, he might tell me not to come. I didn't want to risk that. Not after all this time."

"And what if they're not in Motueka?"

"From what you have told me, there is only one other place — the hospital. We can go there next. Does this work for you?"

"Okay. But once Mom and Dad have got over the shock of seeing me again and meeting you for the first time, I think it's better I leave. You need time with them by yourself. You've an awful lot to catch up on."

For a moment she thought she saw fear in his eyes but reconsidered. This was not a man who showed fear. It was vulnerability.

"What will you do?"

Isobel's face lit up.

"I've rented a car too, so I'll drive to Kaiteriteri. That's a town an hour or so farther up the coast. I emailed my friend Stan to say I was coming back to South Island. Remember, I told you about Stan, the lady with the *moko*?" Isobel made a swirling motion on her chin. "I'll stay there for a day, then call Mom."

Chapter 36

Once again Isobel's heart was racing and her palms sweating as she turned into the Kotara Street and parked opposite number sixty-three. In her rearview mirror she could see Toma's car pulling in behind her. As if on cue, they opened their car doors together.

"That's the house?" he asked.

Isobel nodded. "Are you ready for this?"

He smiled at her. "Thank you for doing this for me. It means more than anything you can imagine."

With a slight straightening of his shoulders, he crossed the road and walked up the driveway with Isobel at his side.

"Okay?" she asked him as her hand reached out to press the buzzer. Toma nodded.

As if the scene from a month ago was being replayed, she heard footsteps approaching the door. It opened. Her mother looked first at Toma, and not recognizing him, shifted her gaze to Isobel. Her eyes widened.

"Isobel? She put her hand to her mouth. "Is it really you?"

Without answering, Isobel stepped over the threshold

and gave her mother a hug. "Yes, Mom. It's me. I'm back. I brought someone to see you and Dad. It's Toma, Dad's brother."

Christina looked past Isobel to the man standing on her doorstep. The recognition came slowly, as if a blurry image was gradually coming into focus.

"Oh my God! It's really you," Christina gasped. "You look so much like him. But...we were told you were dead years ago. I don't understand."

"Christina. I finally get to meet you after all this time."

There was an awkward silence, but before Isobel could interject, Toma spoke again, his voice trembling slightly.

"I am so sorry for all the pain I caused you and Novak. It is all my fault...my stupidity." He gestured towards Isobel. "Isobel found me. She is an amazing..."

Christina finished his sentence. "Daughter. Yes. She *is* an amazing daughter."

She stepped aside to let Toma and Isobel enter the narrow hallway. Before she led them into the sitting room, she paused.

"Isobel has told you about Novak, that he's sick?"

Toma nodded. "Yes. As soon as she told me, I wanted to come."

"He sleeps most of the time now. But his mind is still alert. Come. Come this way."

Toma stood back and let Isobel go first. She followed her mother into the bedroom, noticing that the wheelchair had been pushed against a wall as if it was no longer needed.

Sun poured in the window, highlighting the figure lying on the queen-sized bed. Even in the space of three weeks, Isobel could see the deterioration in her father. He was thinner than before, and his face an ashen gray. His cheeks were hollow, emphasizing the oxygen tube. She approached the bed and leaned in close.

"Dad, it's me. Isobel."

Her father opened his eyes and slowly focused on her face.

"Isobel. I didn't expect to see you again." His voice was a whisper.

"Dad, I've brought someone to see you."

She stepped aside, and Toma moved to the bedside. He said something in a language that Isobel couldn't understand. Her father's response was electrifying. His eyes opened wide as a look of incredulity suffused his face. Then he held his arms out towards his brother, inviting an embrace. Christina touched Isobel's hand gently, pulling her away. Mother and daughter withdrew, both of them weeping. They stood holding hands for a few minutes, listening to the murmur of an unfamiliar language coming from the bedroom.

"I'm going to go now," Isobel said, wiping away tears. "I want Dad and Toma and you to have as much time as possible together. I'll come tomorrow. In the meantime, I'll be at Stan's place if you need me."

"I don't know what to say...."

Christina gave her daughter's hand a squeeze, and Isobel recognized her love in the small gesture.

Chapter 37

On the now-familiar road to Kaiteriteri, Isobel thought back to the first time she had driven this way. It seemed a lifetime ago, and yet it had been barely six weeks. With the exception of three small scars on her abdomen, she looked the same. But in every other sense she had changed. She had found her biological parents. Her mother was dead, the fact irrefutable. But Amela had not abandoned her daughter. And then there was her father, now remarried and with a young son. Her dad was her uncle, and she was pregnant. It sounded like something out of a soap opera. She gave a laugh. She was looking forward to seeing Stan, the one person in the world who could appreciate this comedy of errors.

Stan's Place was closed when she arrived. The note pinned to the door said "Back tomorrow afternoon," so Isobel walked around to the back of the building, through the gate, and into the garden. The door was open. Everything looked exactly as she remembered. There were pieces of outdoor gear in the process of being cleaned or repaired and books and newspapers strewn about on every flat surface. A plate on the kitchen table held the remains of Stan's breakfast and beside it a half-filled mug, the liquid in it now cold. Despite her exhaustion, she tidied up the kitchen, then took the dirty dishes to the sink and washed them. She hadn't the energy to make herself a cup of tea and instead went to her bedroom, carrying the minimum she needed — her wash bag and a change of clothes. On top of the duvet, she found a note: "See you at the Beached Whale later this evening. Stan." Too tired to take a shower, she set her alarm and fell asleep.

~

"So you couldn't stay away, luvvy, eh? I knew I had a magnetic personality."

As soon as Isobel entered the pub, Stan had marched over and rubbed noses with a thoroughly surprised Isobel.

"Even if I do say so, getting rid of your appendix suits you. You look pretty damn healthy. They must have fed you well in that Italian hospital. I think you've put on a bit of weight. Fancy a hike at the weekend? We can do some work on that waistline of yours."

"Sorry Stan, but I'm not allowed carry more than four kilos, and I don't think you want to carry my pack as well as yours."

They both laughed. Stan retrieved her glass from where she had been sitting at the bar waiting for Isobel, and they sat down at a table in the back of the room.

"What are you going to have?" Stan asked, an eye towards the barman, who was waiting to take their order.

"Just a Coca Cola for now, thanks." Isobel said.

Stan pulled back from the table and looked at Isobel critically, her eyes narrowing to slits.

"You're not pregnant, are you?"

Isobel's mouth fell open. "How did you know?"

Stan's eyes glinted. "Magic, eh? We Maori can sense these things." The purple-tinged lips curled downward. "It's not Kauri's, is it?"

"No. The timing is wrong. It's Vic's."

"Just as well then, 'cos he's gone back to his wife and kiddies in Northland.

It was Isobel's turn to look surprised.

"Yes. He's got two kids, a boy and a girl, five and seven, or thereabouts. He just needed a bit of time to sort his head out, so he came to his auntie's place."

She gave Isobel a knowing look. "Seems like a lot of people come to Stan's Place to take stock of themselves. You too?"

Before Isobel could answer, Stan continued, "You didn't have to leave me money for the room the last time. You're *whānau* now. You know — family, like Kauri is. You can come stay anytime."

A lump formed in Isobel's throat, and she took a gulp of her cola.

"So, have you told the lucky guy yet? The keeper?"

"No. He doesn't know yet."

"Mmm. Sounds like he might never know." She lifted an eyebrow. "Have you decided?"

"Not yet." She gave a sigh. "When I found out, I was pretty certain I wasn't going to keep it. I mean, it wasn't planned. But I had a lot of time to think while I was in the hospital. That was a low point, lying there day after day, worrying about everything and with no one to talk to. The doctors weren't sure if they'd have to do a second surgery, and then...then I could have ended up with a colostomy bag."

"But you're good now," Stan said, nodding her head. It was a statement, not a question, and Isobel smiled her agreement.

"How far along are you?"

"Around fifteen weeks. I still have time to make up my mind."

For the next hour Isobel brought Stan up to date on her complicated family dynamics. In the time since they last talked, Isobel's family seemed to have grown exponentially. Stan's *moko* danced at every new revelation.

"That's quite the story," she finally said, catching the barman's eye and signaling for the bill.

"Let me know what you need. Time. Space. Advice. No advice. I can do it all. I'm going to Nelson tonight — sorry, but I promised Meg. I'll be back to open the shop tomorrow morning. In the meantime, make yourself at home."

They stood up and made their way to the exit. Stan climbed into her car and closed the door. Before pulling away, she rolled down the window and said with unaccustomed sincerity, "It's good to have you back."

~

Isobel texted Toma that evening, hoping to find out how the meeting went. His response was immediate, but brief. "Very good. I am going back to Motueka tomorrow morning." She wasn't sure how exhausting it would be for her father to have two visitors in the same day so she texted Toma to let him know she would wait until the following day to visit. After all, the brothers had almost forty years to catch up on.

Chapter 38

Two days later she got a text from Toma. "Call Christina. She needs you."

Instead of calling, Isobel drove to Motueka. When she arrived, her mother hugged her, then led her into the kitchen.

"Your father is sleeping so best not to disturb him for a while. I'll make a cup of tea."

They sat by the large window that overlooked the garden. Spring had arrived, and though it wasn't yet warm enough to sit outside, sun streamed through the window.

"How is Dad?" Isobel asked, looking inquiringly at her mother.

"Not good." Looking down at her hands, Christina fingered her wedding ring. "He's decided not to do any more dialysis."

In the silence that followed, Isobel could hear birds twittering in the shrubbery surrounding the lawn. The kettle began to whistle mournfully and, before the sound could rise to a crescendo, Christina got up and turned it off.

"I suppose you know Toma has gone back to Italy," she

said. Isobel thought she heard a note of relief, or perhaps it was just exhaustion, in her mother's voice.

"No, I didn't know. He didn't tell me." She wasn't sure whether she should be angry or not. It wasn't as if she was going to miss him.

Her mother went over to a small desk, opened a drawer, and took out an envelope.

"He left this for you," she said, handing the letter to Isobel.

She opened it immediately. It contained a single sheet of paper.

Dear Isobel,

Thank you for making it possible for me to see Novak again. It is wonderful to have him back in my life even if the time is short.

I would like to be part of your life in the future but only if you want this.

Toma

Isobel folded the sheet of paper, returned it to the envelope, and slipped it into her purse.

"He wanted to thank me for getting him and Dad together. How did it go, in any case?"

As Christina described it, their reunion had been extraordinary. As much as his strength would allow, Novak had spent most of the past two days talking with Toma. The men had sat for hours together conversing in the language of their childhood.

"I don't know what they talked about. Sometimes they just sat there together in silence. Toma and I did get to talk a little when Novak needed to rest. He's...different. Not like Novak, and then again, at times so very like him."

"What did you talk about?"

"You mostly. And he wanted me to know how grateful he was that we took you all those years ago."

Isobel was silent for a while.

"You have grown into a remarkable young woman," Christina said, her eyes shining. "Even though I had little to do with it, I am so proud of you."

"You and Dad had a lot to do with it. I just didn't see it at the time."

They sat for a while, not needing to talk, each of them absorbed in their own thoughts.

Christina interrupted their reverie. "I think Toma is afraid you won't want to continue having a relationship with him. Will you?"

"I honestly don't know."

"But he's your father."

"No. Novak is my father."

Christina smiled. "Maybe it's okay to have both."

She left the room, returning a few minutes later.

"He's awake now. Go in and see him. I'll warm up a bowl of soup, though he's not very hungry these days."

Isobel went along the corridor and into the bedroom. The shades were drawn, bringing an air of peacefulness to the room. She pulled a chair up to the bedside and took hold of her father's hand.

"Dad. Hi. It's me."

In a faint voice he said, "Isobel. Thank you for coming back. Thank you for finding Toma."

They talked for a little while with Isobel recounting her meeting with Gordana in Sarajevo and filling in the gaps in Toma's narrative.

"I suppose you know he calls himself Paolo Parma now," Isobel said.

"Yes, he told me. I know a little bit about why he changed his name, but it doesn't matter. We are still brothers." Her father smiled. "We talked a lot about our childhood, what we remember of our mother and father, little things like that."

Soon Christina came in with a tray. Isobel changed places so she could feed her husband. He was too weak to do it himself.

"I'll let myself out, Mom. I'll come back tomorrow. I'll call you first."

"Thanks, dear," Christina said, then gave her full attention to her husband.

~

Stan had returned from an overnight hike with two clients, a young couple from England, and readily accepted Isobel's offer to cook dinner, tagliatelle with Italian sausage.

"I was thinking maybe you should go see a gynie to make sure it has all its bits and pieces."

Isobel was standing at the stove stirring the sauce and gave Stan a quizzical look over her shoulder.

"I have absolutely no idea what you are talking about," she said, turning her attention back to the stove.

"G-Y-N-I-E, gynecologist. I know you haven't made up your mind yet. I'd suss it if you had. But it might be a good idea to know what you're dealing with. If the tests come back and they're not good, well, it might make your decision a lot easier."

Isobel said nothing.

"Here, I wrote down the number of the public clinic at the Nelson Hospital."

She pushed a piece of paper across the table, then went back to catching up on the news in the local paper. Isobel considered Stan's suggestion. It was sensible, and it didn't commit her to making a decision — yet. Besides, the clinic was the place she would go if she decided to have an abortion.

~

"You can relax," the doctor informed Isobel after her ultrasound the following day. "Your pregnancy is progressing normally, and your baby should arrive sometime around the middle of April. The ultrasound is inconclusive as to the sex, but we should have the result of the blood test tomorrow. Call me if you want to know." He smiled encouragingly. "Do you want to set up a prenatal schedule here or are you planning to have the baby in the United States?"

Isobel stumbled over her response.

"I...I haven't decided...anything...yet."

~

"You've decided to keep it, haven't you?"

Stan's eyes were wide and there was a trace of a smile on her dark lips. She had just come into the living room from the shop, having closed it up for the day. Isobel was sitting on the couch where, only a month earlier, she and Kauri had enjoyed each other's company. The memory wasn't lost on her each time she sat there or, indeed, each time she climbed into her bed. But like so many pieces of her past, she was learning to let them go.

"Why do you say that?" Isobel asked.

"You've got that look about you," Stan said in a matter-of-fact tone, "Like you had decided to finally get a *moko*." She gave Isobel a crooked smile.

Isobel looked back at her steadily, her face expressionless. Then she broke into a smile.

"Yeah," she said, nodding her head. "I finally made up my mind. It wasn't so much seeing the ultrasound. It's just that finally everything clicked, and I realized I *want* this baby. Plus, I heard from the doctor this morning. All the genetic stuff is good. And I'm going to have a girl."

Saying the words aloud for the first time filled her with an indescribable joy.

"Well, just 'cos you can't celebrate, doesn't mean I'm not going to," Stan said, opening the fridge and taking out a half-full bottle of wine.

"Sure you won't?" she asked, pouring herself a generous glass.

Shaking her head from side to side, Isobel raised her mug. "It's tea for me for the next few months, I'm afraid."

"So, have you told the father yet?"

"No, not yet. I plan to tell them tomorrow when I go to Motueka."

"Not *that* father, you dummy. I mean the real one."

"I haven't decided about Toma. I think I'll wait until the baby comes and see how I feel about him then. He's not been much of a father. Still, he may turn out to be a better grandfather."

Stan threw up her hands in mock frustration. "God, you're thick! I mean the *baby's* father. Remember him? The keeper. Have you told him yet?"

Isobel grimaced.

"No, not yet. It's not the sort of thing you can do in an email, and I don't want to tell him over the phone either. I'm going to wait until I see him. I've been thinking about that too. What if he doesn't want a baby?"

It wasn't a question she expected Stan to answer. All the same, she looked at her expectantly. Stan said nothing.

"Well, I'm prepared to bring the baby up without him, if necessary." Isobel gave a little laugh. "You're right; it *is* a bit like getting a *moko*. There's no going back."

Chapter 39

When Isobel arrived in Motueka the next morning, her mother opened the door immediately as if she had been waiting for her.

"The nurse was here this morning and gave him an injection. He's sleeping now." Her voice cracked. "She said it won't be long."

Isobel hugged her mother, then followed her into the bedroom where they both sat by the bedside. Her father's face was smooth, all of the muscles relaxed. His eyes were closed, but the lids fluttered occasionally. Maybe he is dreaming, Isobel thought, and if so, I hope it is a happy one. Perhaps a dream from his childhood with his younger brother. She took his hand in hers. It felt ridiculously light, like a leaf that had just fallen from a tree, still slightly warm, not yet desiccated.

The previous night Isobel had spent several restless hours considering whether she would tell her parents about the baby now. After all, her father would not be alive by the time she gave birth. As for her mother, Isobel felt unsure. She wanted to tell her but wasn't sure if her mother would welcome a grandchild.

Maggie had been Isobel's grandmother in every sense except DNA, and that relationship had been critical to Isobel being able to move forward with her life. Perhaps Christina might enjoy having a grandchild — someone to boast about with other grandparents without the burden of babysitting? The more Isobel thought about it, the clearer it became.

"Mom, Dad, I'm going to have a baby."

She waited, wondering how her mother would respond to this announcement. Christina turned to her with a look that Isobel couldn't interpret.

"Is it what you want?"

"Yes. It is. I really want this baby."

"Then I am so happy for you, dear. I think you will be a wonderful mother."

Her mother reached out and clasped her hand. Isobel's eyes glistened with tears. She tried to suppress them, brushing them away with her free hand. But the tears continued to fall as she looked at her father. She was about to lose the person she had been closest to throughout her childhood, a gentle man who had tried his best.

"I'm not sure he heard you," Christina said, gesturing towards her husband.

As her mother said this, Isobel felt the faintest pressure on her fingers. A wave of joy flooded through her.

"Dad just squeezed my hand. I think he heard."

Their vigil lasted through to the early afternoon, and then he was gone.

∼

Isobel had stayed with her mother that night. There would be no funeral service, she learned. Novak had not wanted one, nor did he expect Christina to return his ashes to Bosnia. Her mother wasn't sure what she would do with the ashes. Perhaps she might scatter them in the ocean at a later time, but not now.

"I can stay for as long as you like," she offered at breakfast the following morning, but her mother declined.

"It's all right, dear. My sister is driving up from Invercargill tomorrow and will stay for a few weeks. I was thinking I might go back with her."

Isobel had only met Christina's sister once when she came to visit them in Toronto. She was eight at the time, and her recollection was vague. A nice woman with a strange accent who brought candy. Patricia and her husband ran a large farm near Invercargill at the southernmost tip of South Island, giving them little opportunity to get away. When Christina emigrated to Canada, the two sisters promised each other they would meet in person every ten years. Ten years after that visit, Isobel was in college in Wisconsin. Since coming back to New Zealand, it was easier for the two sisters to get together, although with Novak's illness it had become more of a challenge. Nonetheless, they spoke on the phone every Sunday morning.

"Will you go back to Invercargill for good?"

"No, dear. I like it here in Motueka. For one thing the weather is a lot nicer than down south. Besides, I have good friends here." She looked at her daughter affectionately.

"I'll be here when you come back to visit with Vic and the baby. And if you need me sooner, I'll come to you."

Chapter 40

Stan looked at Isobel's face when she walked into the shop. Isobel's eyes bore the evidence of recent tears, which told Stan everything she needed to know without asking the obvious question. Stan came over and put her arms around her. It felt a little awkward — they had never touched before. Still, Isobel appreciated the gesture. After a few seconds she straightened, withdrawing from Stan's embrace.

"At least I got to tell Dad I'm going to have a baby. I think he heard. He squeezed my hand. Of course, that might have meant something else but I'm taking it as a positive sign." She gave a little laugh. "Mom surprised me. I think she might like the idea of being a grandmother. Ten thousand miles away from the kid makes it a lot easier of course. All the same, she offered to come to the States if I need her. I never expected that."

"Would you ask her?"

Isobel considered Stan's question for a few moments before answering.

"I honestly don't know. It's not as if she hasn't had experience with a baby. She had me, after all, and she said I was a colicky baby. She was a nurse before I came along and went back to it again when I went to school. I suspect she'd be quite good. She was wonderful with Dad."

Isobel gave a long sigh. She had no tears left for now, and mourning would have to wait. There were more important issues, like going home and telling Vic he was about to become a father.

∼

On Isobel's last night in Kaiteriteri, she and Stan went across the road to the Beached Whale one last time. Stan was taking a tour group to Abel Tasman the following morning so there would be little time for farewells the next day.

"I'm going to miss this when I get home," Isobel said, looking greedily at the basket of piping hot fish and chips that had been placed in front of her at their regular table in the back of the bar.

"Yeah, right. We know the good stuff — deep-fried fish 'n' spuds," Stan said, raising one eyebrow.

Isobel laughed. There was a new lightness to her. She felt like an insect that had just shed its pupal case and was finally unfolding its wings, ready for adult flight. Returning to New Zealand with Toma had enabled this feeling of equanimity and allowed it to sink into her core. No matter what happened in the future, she was certain she would manage. With a mental nod to Maggie, for she no longer felt in need of a full-blown conversation, she dug into her basket of chips and ate ravenously.

"Oh. I almost forgot," Isobel said when she had finished every morsel of her meal. "It'll be fall in Wisconsin when I get there. When I left it was still summer, so I've nothing warm to wear. Any chance I could check out the locker and see if there's a coat that'll fit me? I'm happy to pay you."

"No need to pay me anything. Take anything you find. You can always bring it back the next time you come. I know you'll be back. And it's not like the coat will have gone out of fashion." Stan gave a belly laugh.

Isobel licked the last traces of salt and grease from her fingers. She noticed Stan's face becoming serious, the sides of her mouth turning down, emphasizing the spirals of her *moko*. The scimitars were about to clash.

"You *will* come back soon, won't you? I want to meet the newcomer," she said, pointing to Isobel's belly, which was beginning to round out. "And bring that guy of yours. I want to see what a male keeper is like, especially since I've never met one yet."

Isobel had been waiting for the right time to ask.

"Is there such a thing as a godmother in Maori? You know what I mean, don't you? It's not that I expect you to take her if anything happened to me. God knows what would happen if she hung out with you!"

They both laughed.

"I just want her to know there's someone amazing looking out for her even if you're on the other side of the world."

"Like a *fairy* godmother?" Stan roared with laughter at her own witticism. "Actually, there is a Maori term for a fairy godmother. It's *te pouaka wahine*. The literal translation is something like this." She cupped her hands beneath her breasts and gave them a shake. "But the sentiment is more or less what you're getting after. The answer is yes — I'd be honored to be her godmother."

"She's the one who'll be honored," Isobel replied, tapping her belly gently.

Chapter 41

In the shop at Auckland Airport's international terminal, Isobel saw a copy of the book she had left behind at the Ljubljana bus terminal. While the title was the same, the book had a different cover, and she opened it to make sure it was Keri Hulme's *The Bone People*. Satisfied, she turned to the next page and read the dedication, which she had skipped over previously. It read, "Motueka, 1966 — Moeraki & Okarito, 1978," which she could only presume were the start and end of the author's writing journey. The symmetry was not lost on her. Motueka had been the start of her journey too. She paid for the book and slipped it into her backpack.

Isobel had much to think about on the long journey home. These weren't new thoughts. They had been lurking in the recesses of her mind, successfully avoided until the conversation she had with Stan before leaving New Zealand. She had no doubts about the baby. But Vic? A warm feeling came over her as she visualized his smile once he caught sight of her at Dane County Regional Airport. His genuine joy at having her back safely, back in his life, would be hard to resist. But she had changed. Distance had allowed her to see their relationship in a different light. All the positives about Vic were still there. He was kind, hardworking, reliable, loving; she had absolutely no doubt that he loved her. But there were negatives too. Like many thirty-year-old Midwestern men saddled with the genes of their Norwegian and German forebears, he had a certain way of looking at life. He had disapproved of her going to New Zealand. To an extent it was a need for control; she understood that for she herself had the same tendency. Her departure had upset his predictable life, and he was someone who didn't adapt well to change. While she was in New Zealand, their conversations had always come around to what was going wrong in *his* life — work pressures, money, and dealing with Lara's accusations. True, he had offered to come to Verona, but he had given in readily when she argued against it. Was she being fair to him? How would she have behaved had it been Vic who left her to follow an ill-defined odyssey?

She dragged her mind back to practicalities. She still had eight thousand dollars left from the money Maggie put into her bank account. Vic owed her ten thousand, and she had another twelve in savings. Reluctantly she realized that the money Maggie left her for vet school, two hundred thousand dollars, might not be used for that purpose. Instead, it would give her a freedom that few women in her position experienced. She and her daughter could live comfortably for the next few years as a family unit of two. If she chose to work, she was sure she could get her old job back at the veterinary clinic, or even go back to being a school counselor. But neither of those jobs would satisfy her for the rest of her life. She wanted more.

She remembered that sinking feeling as she left the veterinary school building the day she learned it was too late to get a deferment. Realistically, by the time she got home, it would be too late to assemble and submit an application to veterinary school. Even if she was accepted, she knew it would be impossible to concentrate on her studies with a new baby. Perhaps in a year or two she would be in a better position to balance motherhood and a rigorous four-year academic program. As if on cue, a conversation she had with Maggie the previous year came to mind. Maggie had always stressed the importance of a back-up plan, and as a result Isobel had also applied to the master's of public health program as well as vet school. With her background and experience, she was seen as an ideal candidate and quickly accepted. Thinking about it now, Isobel remembered that the MPH curriculum could be completed on a part-time basis. Applications were not due until January, giving her more than enough time. It all came back to Maggie.

Just then the airplane hit a patch of turbulence. Isobel cinched her seatbelt carefully under the small bulge. Her thoughts shifted abruptly from career plans to the baby and then to the baby's father. Whether or not their relationship survived, Vic would want to be involved in his daughter's life. He was that sort of person. Without question he would pay child support. Would he offer to marry her, she wondered? The more important question was: did she want to marry him?

Over the past couple of weeks, she had considered starting a new life in New Zealand. She could have faded from Vic's life, and he would never know about the baby. But the idea of depriving him of his daughter was unconscionable. Even Toma had recognized how much he had missed by being absent from Isobel's childhood. Her daughter would have to forego being a Kiwi, but she would have American as well as a Canadian citizenship, giving her access to much of the world when she grew up. Isobel smiled inwardly. Maggie had taught her well — back-up plans for the next generation too.

Chapter 42

The wintry sky was an iridescent blue as they crossed over Lake Mendota and approached Dane County Regional Airport. The plane touched down, taxied to the terminal building, and came to a halt with a slight lurch, a signal for passengers around her to begin tapping on their cell phones. Isobel retrieved her backpack from under the seat. Pulling on the coat she had borrowed from Stan, an anorak that came to her knees, she braced herself. Whatever happened, she was going to be okay.

"Wish you were here, Maggie," she mouthed silently.

Vic was waiting at the bottom of the escalator. She had forgotten how tall he was and that he held one of his shoulders slightly lower than the other. His smile hadn't changed though, nor his embrace. He pulled her tightly to his chest, murmuring into her ear, "I have missed you so much. So much."

"Careful," she said, pushing back from him.

"Sorry. Sorry. I forgot completely about the surgery. Does it hurt much?"

Isobel answered truthfully, "A little. At times."

He put his arm around her shoulder and gave her a gentle squeeze. "Better?"

"Yeah." She gave him a warm smile. "We need to pick up my bag. I decided to check it through so as not to have to lift it into the overhead compartment."

As they walked to Vic's pickup truck in the parking ramp, he stopped and turned to her.

"Let me give you a proper kiss this time." His eyes were shining.

The kiss was long and slow and lingering, and despite standing on a chilly concrete ramp, Isobel allowed herself to be loved again by this man. All her lies of omission and commission were in the past, never to be confessed. Only one remained, and she would wait until they got home to confess that one.

"Have you heard anything from the lawyer recently?" she asked when they had paid the parking fee and were on their way.

Vic slapped the steering wheel with the palm of his hand. His voice was exultant.

"You won't believe it. I think she's gone."

"What do you mean, gone?"

"Well, Richard brought the stuff to the DNA place in Madison that Gordana suggested. He was a bit weirded-out collecting the toothbrush from the bathroom and all that. But he went along with it. I suppose he's watched enough crime dramas on TV. After a week or so when he hadn't heard from Lara's lawyer, he called the guy. Seems that Grace Mangan has disappeared. She hasn't responded to emails or the letter he sent by registered mail. The phone number she gave him is no longer in service. She hasn't paid the guy either. Even though he didn't say it outright, he made it pretty clear to Richard that he thinks it was all a con."

Vic's smile disappeared. He looked towards Isobel, guilt written all over his face.

"I feel badly about this, but I read the letters Lara wrote to Maggie. Maggie didn't hide them or anything; they were lying on the desk in the study. Maybe she wanted us to read them. Did you know Lara was asking Maggie for money constantly? In every single letter — there must have been about five or six of them — she'd ask for a few thousand dollars each time. And Maggie sent it. It's all there in her checkbook. I looked."

His shame-faced expression was replaced by a look of sadness. "I can't believe it, that Maggie was so gullible, I mean."

"I had a suspicion that was happening," Isobel said. "In the beginning I was so pleased they were writing to each other. But the thing is, Maggie never seemed overjoyed when a letter came. I often picked up her mail, especially towards the end, and I could recognize Lara's handwriting."

"Yeah. Well, now you know why."

They drove in silence for a few minutes, each of them thinking about how cruel this mother-daughter reunion had been.

"I didn't think it was right to give the letters to Richard, but I gave him Maggie's checkbook. That way he has a record of the payments. It must have totaled over fifteen thousand dollars."

Isobel gave a little shiver.

"I'm mad at myself for having found Lara, but in a funny way I'm not mad at Lara herself. After all, if it hadn't been for her, Maggie would have left us sooner. She'd have taken her life when she went to Ireland after Christmas. Because of Lara, you and I got an extra six months with her."

"I wonder did she suspect Lara was conning her?"

"Maybe she did. Maybe she gave Lara the money out of guilt — guilt for the real Lara, I mean. Maggie's real daughter is still out there somewhere."

～

They were approaching Maggie's place. No matter that Vic owned it now, it would always be "Maggie's place" as far as Isobel was concerned. The long driveway with its border of tall red pines brought back memories of the first time she had come here. Expecting to find a large house at the end of such a formal avenue, Isobel had been taken aback by the unprepossessing log cabin and rickety barn. She had been late for her interview with Maggie, who she had been warned was a formidable lady. Her heart had been pounding in her chest that time. This time she felt something different, a tiny flutter in her belly.

They drove up to the cabin, and Vic turned off the engine.

"Why are we stopping here?" Isobel asked, expecting him to drive around to the guesthouse.

"I have a surprise for you," he said. He gave her an enigmatic smile.

They walked into the kitchen and for a moment Isobel was disoriented. The room looked the same, inasmuch as the whitewashed log walls were still there, as was the counter that bisected the room and separated the working area from the kitchen table. Vic stood beside her, waiting for her to say something.

"You got a new fridge," she said. Walking over to it, she opened the shiny, stainless steel double doors. No longer would it be necessary to stoop to retrieve food from the interior.

"Yes. And that's not all. We've got a new countertop, a new sink, and best of all, new flooring with in-floor heating. No more baseboard electric heaters. I had to literally dig out the old floor by hand. There was no other way. The logs underneath were resting directly on dirt. No wonder Maggie had such a huge heating bill."

His enthusiasm was infectious.

"You're wonderful," she said, coming back to where he stood and kissing him.

"This is what I've been doing all the time you were away. I'd come home after work, grab a bite to eat, then come here with Oliver and work until midnight, later some nights." He pointed to one of the whitewashed walls. "Remember the fieldstone rocks that supported that log wall? I jacked up the logs and replaced them with concrete. I've put some of the fieldstone back so it looks the same, but now it's tight. No more drafts, and it won't bulge or sag with frost heaves. I haven't got around to repainting the walls yet, but next week I should be able to finish."

His look, a mixture of pride and love, made her heart swell. It shocked her that only a short while ago she had considered staying in New Zealand and not telling him about the baby. Now, feeling his arm around her, she was sure that no matter what happened next, he would always be there for her.

"I have a surprise for you too," she said, a tiny note of caution in her voice.

She unzipped her parka and opened it, placing her hand on her belly.

"I'm pregnant." She gave him an apologetic smile. "I know you weren't expecting this, and it's okay if you don't want… if you're not ready to be a father. I can do it by myself, and I would understand completely. We've never really talked about having a baby, but the thing is, it happened. I could have done something about it and not told you. But I've had a lot of time to think about it over the past two months. And this is what I want."

Vic stared at her for a minute or more. She could almost see his brain taking in the information, turning it this way and that as he tried to fit it into his mind, his life. He swallowed a couple of times, nodding as if to shake away the tears that had formed in his eyes. For a moment he didn't say anything, just pulled her to him gently. Then she heard him whisper, "I'm going to be a dad." He said it again, louder this time, his voice ringing with delight, "I'm going to be a dad."

"It's a girl. I thought we'd call her Maggie Amela Wagner," Isobel said.

They stood for a few minutes, neither of them wanting to disturb the perfection of the moment.

Vic pulled away reluctantly. "I'll be back in a minute. I just need to let Oliver out. He'll have heard the truck and wonder why I haven't come in yet."

As he turned to leave, his hand trailed over her belly. He was beaming.

Isobel stood in the room where she had first met Maggie O'Connor. She looked out towards the barn in time to see a joyous streak of brown fur rounding the corner and racing up to the cabin. Vic followed the dog at a measured pace, strong and steady as she knew he would always be. The first time she stood in this spot she had felt abandoned, first by her biological parents and then by her adoptive parents. She had agreed to work for Maggie because she hated her job and wasn't sure what to do next. That year had changed everything. It had given her a new purpose and brought Vic into her life. Sadly, it had taken Maggie away, but her death had enabled Isobel to reconcile with her past. And now she had been given another gift, one that to her surprise, she found she couldn't refuse. Now she had a family, more diverse and complex than most, yet full of people who would be there for her, always.

THE END

Why would Maggie O'Connor give Isobel
such a life-changing gift?
Pick up the companion book: *A Measured Thread*,
to read the compelling story.

Acknowledgments

When I finished writing *A Measured Thread*, it seemed like a good time to part company with my protagonist, Maggie O'Connor. Still, I couldn't help thinking about her young companion, Isobel Babić. I wanted Isobel to figure out what she wanted out of life. It took her (and me) a few years, but I'm happy to say she is going to be okay.

Two wonderful writing companions and NaNoWriMo (National Novel Writing Month) were the impetus for finishing the first draft of *Finding Isobel*. Valerie Biel and Silvia Acevedo, you are the best writing partners anyone could have. Thank you for keeping me on track and also for your superb skills as beta readers. Three other beta readers gave me excellent feedback, and I am so grateful for their input. William Ried, Chad Guenther, and Courtney Guenther, you are the best. Every novel needs a skilled editor and ChristineKeleny is just that. This is my fourth time working with Christine and it's a pleasure every time.

Encouragement comes in all forms. The Crossroads yoga and coffee group in Cross Plains, Wisconsin, is every writer's dream. I hope Isobel doesn't disappoint them. Friends and family constantly ask "How's the writing going?" and while I don't always feel positive, they give me the impetus to get back to work.

The Wisconsin Writers Association is a constant source of inspiration and help. The critique group they organized, led by the unparalleled Laurie Scheer, was a wonderful experience. Thank you Bert Kreitlow, Cara Salazar, Rosemary Potter, Ted Fearson, Lee Cantillon, Rebecca Ottinger, and Kim Mullen Kuehl. I learned so much from all of you.

The book club I've been meeting with for several years are all accomplished writers, which makes our monthly get-togethers not just fun but also a valuable sounding board. Thank you to Chris Clay, Mary Clay, Caryn Wadler, Roxanne Aehl, Madhu Singh, Barbara Lobermeier, and Kathy Steffen.

I worried about a cover design for the novel before it dawned on me that Gina Hecht, whose beautiful landscape painting became the cover for *A Measured Thread*, would be the perfect person to create a cover for *Finding Isobel*. Unbeknownst to me, she had titled a recent painting of hers "Finding Joy." The stars were aligned.

Last, and so deserving of thanks are my first writing partner, my sister Valerie Behan, and my constant love, my husband, Tim Heggland.

About the Author

MARY BEHAN is a former professor of neuroscience. Now retired, she devotes her time to writing fiction, memoir, and short stories. Her first book, *Abbey Girls*, is a memoir she wrote with her sister, Valerie Behan, about their childhood in Ireland. Her debut novel, *A Measured Thread*, set in Wisconsin and Ireland, was named a Top 100 Indie Book in 2020, a finalist in the Page Turner Awards, and an eLit medal winner. *Kernels*, a collection of short stories, was published in 2021 and is a 2022 Shelf Unbound Best Indie award winner. Her stories have been published in the Irish literary journal, *Crossways*, and received Honorable Mention in the Writer's Digest Writing Competition. Mary lives with her husband in the Driftless Area of southwest Wisconsin. Visit her at mvbehan.com.

∼

If you enjoyed this book, please consider leaving a review on your favorite website (Amazon, Goodreads...). Reviews are incredibly helpful to indie-authors like Mary.

www.ingramcontent.com/pod-product-compliance
Lightning Source LLC
LaVergne TN
LVHW041625060526
838200LV00040B/1436

9 781734 494365